# Looking for Love in Faraway Places
## *Tales of Gay Men's Romance Overseas*

Michael T. Luongo
Editor

**HPP**

Harrington Park Press®
The Trade Division of The Haworth Press, Inc.
New York • London • Oxford

For more information on this book or to order, visit
http://www.haworthpress.com/store/product.asp?sku=5366

or call 1-800-HAWORTH (800-429-6784) in the United States and Canada
or (607) 722-5857 outside the United States and Canada

or contact orders@HaworthPress.com

Published by

Harrington Park Press®, the trade division of The Haworth Press, Inc., 10 Alice Street, Binghamton, NY 13904-1580.

PUBLISHER'S NOTE
The development, preparation, and publication of this work has been undertaken with great care. However, the Publisher, employees, editors, and agents of The Haworth Press are not responsible for any errors contained herein or for consequences that may ensue from use of materials or information contained in this work. The Haworth Press is committed to the dissemination of ideas and information according to the highest standards of intellectual freedom and the free exchange of ideas. Statements made and opinions expressed in this publication do not necessarily reflect the views of the Publisher, Directors, management, or staff of The Haworth Press, Inc., or an endorsement by them.

Although the stories in this collection are nonfiction, identities and circumstances of individuals included in this book have been changed to secure confidentiality.

Cover design by Kerry Mack.
TR: 11.06.06

### Library of Congress Cataloging-in-Publication Data

Looking for love in faraway places : tales of gay men's romance overseas / Michael T. Luongo, editor.
      p. cm.
   ISBN-13: 978-1-56023-697-9 (alk. paper)
   ISBN-10: 1-56023-697-3 (alk. paper)
   ISBN-13: 978-1-56023-539-2 (pbk. : alk. paper)
   ISBN-10: 1-56023-539-X (pbk. : alk. paper)
   1. Gay men—Fiction. 2. Gay men's writings, American. 3. Short stories, American.
I. Luongo, Michael.
PS648.H57L66 2007
813'.60832—dc22
                                                                        2006022946

*Michael T. Luongo, Editor*

# Looking for Love
# in Faraway Places
## *Tales of Gay Men's*
## *Romance Overseas*

*Pre-publication
REVIEWS,
COMMENTARIES,
EVALUATIONS . . .*

"Travel, like love, is perilous, surprising, exhausting, rewarding, and ultimately necessary for those souls looking to gain new perspectives of self and home. So it's doubly interesting that editor Michael T. Luongo would gather stories that combine the two, love and travel, inviting writers to expose their explorations overseas, in deserts, on beaches, in cold cities, and on warm islands. And if the language of love does not always translate well then what sometimes can't be said can certainly be felt, remembered, and shared. So many travel guides are designed to make us feel either safe or at least well-informed. Thankfully this book offers no maps, just a collection of stories that widens the definition of the gay experience past a few American metropolises, touching on issues from marriage rights to immigration and terrorism, all while keeping a smart eye on an irrefutable fact: the heart's wings will take it wherever it wants to go. In that sense the best stories in *Looking for Love in Faraway Places* fly and fly high."

**Tom Cardamone**
*Novelist and Editor*

# Looking for Love
# in Faraway Places
## *Tales of Gay Men's*
## *Romance Overseas*

*HARRINGTON PARK PRESS*®
*Out in the World*
Michael T. Luongo
Editor

*Looking for Love in Faraway Places: Tales of Gay Men's Romance Overseas* edited by Michael T. Luongo

*Gay Travels in the Muslim World* edited by Michael T. Luongo

*You Can Run: Gay, Glam, and Gritty Travels in South America* by Jesse Archer

Some unusual circumstances in the making of this book call
for some unusual notes here in the dedication. On a happy note,
I want to say, as was my original intention, for L.W. and L.F.
in Buenos Aires, a happy 25th. You both are the epitome
of a couple who found love in a faraway place.

But I must also add a dedication with sad reflection for
M.S. Hunter, the author of "Samoa Memories," and for Richard D.
Thompson, author of "Blue Asia," both of whom died during the
editing of this book. Best thoughts to them and their families
and special friends they both made on trips around the world up
until the very ends of their lives. The both of you will also
be an inspiration for me until I too take the ultimate
and final trip of my life.

# CONTENTS

Preface:  A Note from the Editor                                    ix

Acknowledgments                                                     xv

Chapter 1. Friends, Roman, and Countrymen                           1
    *Marc J. Heft*

Chapter 2. My Canterbury Tale or the House in Broadstairs          17
    *Michael T. Luongo*

Chapter 3. Blue Asia                                               29
    *Richard D. Thompson*

Chapter 4. Running with the Bull: A Madrid Romance                 39
    *Gabriel Schael*

Chapter 5. Journey to the End of the Land                          55
    *Morris Kafka*

Chapter 6. Marcelo                                                 67
    *Michael Mele*

Chapter 7. Costumes, Customs, and One Camaro                       75
    *Ken Baehr*

Chapter 8. Paradox                                                 89
    *Thomas Bradbury*

Chapter 9. Samoa Memories                                          97
    *M. S. Hunter*

Chapter 10. The Shosholoza Meyl: Johannesburg
    to Cape Town                                103
    *Des Ariel*

Chapter 11. The Broken Promise                                117
        *Dayton Estes*

Chapter 12. The Ukimwi Road                                   129
        *Richard Burnett*

Chapter 13. Trying to Stop Water with a Net                   137
        *James W. Jones*

About the Editor                                              149

Contributors                                                  151

# Preface: A Note from the Editor

It begins as love always does: A casual glance, a smile on the edge of the mouth, a laugh of recognition when you realize he is doing the same. It's only the setting that's different. Maybe it's some faraway tropical island, the hot sand under your feet, trying to communicate in a language you barely understand. Perhaps it's a European capital where crowned heads once plotted global conquest in a far less peaceful way than you are right now. Sometimes, though, it's just the other coast, or a heartland city your boss sends you to. No matter where it is, when love strikes far away, it's always different from when love strikes at home.

*Looking for Love in Faraway Places* is a collection of stories as varied as the continents. The men who have contributed, nearly all American-born, have found love in such exotic locales as Latin America, Asia, and all across Europe. Others found romance closer to home, just above the border in Canada, or in the Northeast United States.

What makes these relationships different are the special challenges that come with them. Gay men's love lives are already complicated enough, let alone finding love in a faraway place. These relationships must be sustained via telephone calls or with expensive trips cross-country or across the ocean. Even beyond these challenges, sometimes governments work against same-sex love, as in the case of Gabriel Schael's "Running with the Bull: A Madrid Romance" or James W. Jones's "Trying to Catch Water with a Net." In a post–9/11 world, Homeland Security is doing all it can to hurt anyone with a foreign accent. Without the legal protection of marriage that straights have, gay men and lesbians are in the worst position when it comes to trying to keep an overseas relationship together.

*Looking for Love in Faraway Places*
© 2007 The Haworth Press, Inc. All rights reserved.
doi:10.1300/5366_a

Schael's story is also pulled along by the cultural clashes between men who grew up in very different worlds—one in Los Angeles, and one in Madrid. These same cultural clashes are a major factor for many of the other men whose stories appear in this collection. Sometimes love is enough to overcome these clashes, and sometimes, it is not. Such is the case for Marc Heft in his story "Friends, Roman, and Countrymen." Even something as seemingly simple as a reference to an American television sitcom would throw off a night out for Marc when out on the town with his Czech boyfriend.

The differences run far deeper for Thomas Bradbury, who is using a pen name, in his story "Paradox." In this story the cultural challenge is the very meaning of what it is to be gay when his lover is a married Turkish man with children and everyone in the family seems to know what is going on. Gay love overseas becomes redefined in this case within the context of another culture. It is these differences, the kinds of love that you can't find in Chelsea, West Hollywood, or even Des Moines for that matter, that make the relationship all the more meaningful for some of the gay men in this collection.

Sometimes love overseas is simply about being in a certain place at a certain time in one's life. It's not about seeking out love overseas as a special mission, but is simply about being away and falling in love after a chance encounter. Such was the case for Dayton Estes in "The Broken Promise." As a young man in early 1960's Germany, a relationship somehow oddly found its way to him. "Samoa Memories" tells of a similar situation, which manifests itself almost unintentionally and by accident of discovery. The author, M. S. Hunter, was based on the island nation for a year. Instead of one man, however, the entire island of sensual men and their escapades become the focus of his attention. This story also represents a sad case for me as an editor. M. S. Hunter, known to his friends as Max, and with a real name of Frank A. Rhuland Jr., died during the making of this book. This Massachusetts native did two of the things he enjoyed to the end: he wrote and he traveled, dying on July 2, 2004, in Honduras. Thanks to his sister Amy Rhuland Davis I was able to include his wonderful, sexy but sensitive, and funny work in this collection. I am grateful to her, and am honored as an editor. As it is with Hunter, so, unfortunately, it is with Richard D. Thompson, who also died during the book's creation. A native of Idaho who had moved to California, he passed away on March 9, 2005. Through this experience, however, I was able to get to know his mother Gloria Martin, and I am forever grateful to her as well for allowing me to publish her son's work. One of these days in my own travels I will get to meet both Amy and Gloria in person.

My previous book with The Haworth Press was called *Between the Palms: A Collection of Gay Travel Erotica*. I have to admit that it was much easier to get people to submit for that collection than it was for this one. Although you'll find in this book a few of the same authors from *Between the Palms,* and some stories here with their own erotic element, it was much harder to get men to contribute to this collection. This is perhaps because love far away, as opposed to simply sex far away, seems to hit us a little deeper, becoming something all that more difficult to write. A common response from many of the people I asked to contribute was that they would have to ask their partners, that it was not just about themselves that they would be writing but also about the person closest to them. It was a surprise to me how hard it was to put this book together because of the fear so many writers have of bringing their loved ones into a story. Some authors, such as Des Ariel, who is also using a pen name, worried because the stories they are telling are not happy ones, they are stories in which the love they looked for overseas and at a tremendous personal cost simply did not work out. For some of the authors in the collection, their lives are forever changed as AIDS—still a defining feature in the gay community—takes away the men they have called the loves of their lives.

My own story, "My Canterbury Tale or the House in Broadstairs," is a case in which I worried about hurting the closeted man with whom I once shared a very odd relationship. I doubt he will ever come across this book by accident, and his name has been changed as well, but still I wonder and worry. For myself, though, the hardest part, and one that makes me understand the fears of some of my authors, is that I also admit not simply the problems I saw in my partner but the problems within myself that I needed to overcome, the problems that kept me in the relationship. Sometimes when we live overseas, even in a country that speaks the same language, we can be overwhelmed and lonely. Like the boats in the foggy harbor my British lover and I could see from the window from our hideaway, I needed something to moor myself to when I felt lost living overseas. He was what I chose in that moment and place. I can't say it was wrong or right of me, it simply was. I'll leave you to read and be the judge.

Though my time in England was perhaps the most anchored I have ever been with a man in another country, I have fallen in love overseas many times. As a free bird that loves to travel and does so with tremendous frequency, the idea of a man in a place far away is something I can think about when life at home in New York fills me with the monotony of the ordinary. I now understand the electric sensations the heroines of Victorian novels felt when the postman came by with letters from their clandestine lovers who were pulled away to far-flung parts of the British Empire. When I daydream about any of these men I have met around the world—in France, Argentina, Cuba, and so many other places—I know he's just a phone call or an e-mail away, and I can imagine being in his arms once again, and the romance floods over me once more. Even in my daydreams the loves I have found in other countries fill me with a passion I can't find at home. I often wonder, though, if my feelings would be the same if I lived every day in the same city as these men. Would I instead be filled with boredom, oppressed by the routine? Even in romantic Paris we'd still have to do the laundry and go grocery shopping. Love, no matter how strong, won't do it for us.

Yet for some men I know a lifelong love overseas can be achieved. One of the sweetest stories I know of two men who found this are friends of mine in Buenos Aires. One is a Brit, the other an Argentine who met at the dawn of the 1980s, just before the Falkland Islands War. As a new Queen Elizabeth's armada made its way to humiliate yet another Spanish-speaking country the Brit worried about living in Argentina and being considered an enemy of the nation. Still, in spite of war and separation, these two strong hearts found their way back to each other. They'll soon celebrate their silver anniversary. The two are an example of the extreme political, cultural, and emotional challenges gay men have to overcome to stay together.

Yet, it's no easier now in twenty-first-century America. During the preparation of this book, I did an article in *Out Traveler* magazine looking at the legal issues for gays and lesbians who fall in love overseas or with travelers who visit the United States. Oddly, according to Immigration Equality, an organization that helps gay immigrants, the legalization of same-sex unions in Europe, Canada, and other countries, as well as the very possibility of gay marriage's legalization in certain U.S. states, has made it all the harder for gays and lesbians to sustain an overseas relationship. In a hardened post–9/11 world, two men's declaration of love across the borders is a message to Uncle Sam that someone might try to overstay a visa, skip a return flight home, or try to work illegally just to be with the one he loves. In these cases it is our own country that becomes the terrorist state, torturing the souls of men who simply want to love each other.

This marriage issue and its method of making gay men feel like second-class citizens continues to be fought everywhere in the United States, coast to coast, from the beaches of New Jersey where I grew up, to upstate New York, to the Midwest, to the marble steps of San Francisco's city hall. Straight people fall in love with people from overseas too, but they get to bring them home without shame or hiding. We don't. Love may know no boundaries, but the law as it stands certainly does.

Why shouldn't those of us who found love overseas have as many rights as the straight couple who does the same? For now the fight is for all of us to have this right, the right to love as we wish or not to love at all. The battle continues for recognition in the eyes of the law, even if hearts know they need no one to tell them what to do. Hearts will do as they please. If time, distance, and the eternal unwavering sea can not keep two people apart, why does something as mutable as the law, based on the whim and prejudices of silly men and women, think it can? Love, after all, whether found far away or close to home, is the greatest voyage of all.

# Acknowledgments

I want to first thank Jay Quinn for working with me once again, and to Rebecca and Robert for always so quickly answering my numerous silly questions. A big thanks also goes out of course to Bill Cohen and to Bill Palmer for working with me on the ideas behind getting this book into print. As usual, thanks to my roommates Harry and Khoa for putting up with my late-night editing habits and pacing, and for keeping track of my mail when I travel.

Thanks to Ingrid for always listening to my editing worries for this and so many other books and articles, and thanks to Gisele, who knows so well herself about looking for love in faraway places. I hope you find the love you deserve here in New York. For Matthew for asking me to write about overseas love for *Out Traveler,* some of which helped form my editor's note for this book. Thanks also to him for help with Polynesian words. A million thanks go to Florence Amy Rhuland Davis, M. S. Hunter's sister, for working with me on making sure her brother's story got into print. You are so wonderful, and I have enjoyed our phone conversations. I only wish we knew each other under better circumstances. For the same reasons I thank Ms. Gloria Martin, Richard Thompson's mother, whom I met also through strange and trying circumstances. You must be very proud of your son. I am honored to have his work in this collection.

# ❧ 1    Friends, Roman, and Countrymen

*Marc J. Heft*

I boarded the number 16 tram in front of my apartment on Chrudimska Street in Vinohrady, a trendy neighborhood in central Prague. It was a crisp autumn morning in October and a rally to legalize gay partnerships was being held in Namesti Miru, one of the city's main squares. Since I was teaching English and living in the Czech Republic I thought it was important to participate in the social changes sweeping this former communist satellite state. Of course, that's a load of crap—I just wanted an excuse to meet cute Czech boys.

When I arrived at the square everyone was in full rally mode. Gay couples and straight couples were all enjoying their newfound semi-freedom. I walked through the crowd looking for my friends, and that's when I spotted him. Roman was stunning, he was six foot two with a shaved head, black glasses, and built like a linebacker with shoulders that reached all the way to Sudetenland. No time to be timid.

I approached him, trying to think of a good opening line, when it didn't come to me I fell back on the old standard: *"Mluvite anglicky?"* (Do you speak English?)

His smile was incredible. "Yes, I do."

"What does the banner on the front of the stage say?"

"Legalize gay partnerships now."

I know he answered me, but, for a moment, I was so stunned to be talking to him I could barely remember what he said.

*"Jemenjuje se Marc."* (My name is Marc.)

*"Jemenuje se Roman."* (My name is Roman.)


*Looking for Love in Faraway Places*
© 2007 The Haworth Press, Inc. All rights reserved.
doi:10.1300/5366_01

"You speak Czech?"

*"Jenom trochu."* (Only a little.)

"Your pronunciation is excellent."

A compliment—he's interested.

Roman was thirty-two and worked for a prominent Czech bank. He was smart, polite, really good-looking, and clearly wanted to continue our conversation. We spent the next two hours talking and flirting. It was one of those great life moments, one of those moments when I remembered why I was living abroad, one of those moments it was just great to be alive.

Then the lesbians showed up.

Juliet, Denisa, Klara, Marketa, and a few more thrown in for good measure. Why did they always travel in packs? Denisa ran up, tackled me, and in her sexy *The Unbearable Lightness of Being* voice said, "Hello Daddy." She found it very amusing that she was twenty and I was thirty-eight—old enough to be her father. I got to my feet, regained my composure, and tried not to look too flustered. I introduced Roman to the rampaging lesbian horde. I really did like these girls, but at the moment I just wanted them to go away. I was sending my message to Juliet via the obvious "go away" stare I had locked on her, and being the clever girl that she was, she got it.

"We'll be back in a few minutes—I see someone I know," Juliet said, and then added, "We're meeting the girls from my hockey team at a pub near the river. You're coming, right?"

I looked at Roman as if to say "Please give me a reason not to, say that you would rather I go with so you can keep me locked in your bedroom for the next week or so." Unfortunately, that didn't happen; he just stood there smiling politely.

"Would you like to join me, Juliet, and a dozen or so Czech lesbian hockey players for a drink?" Who could resist such a tempting offer?

"I'd like to but I have to be somewhere in a little while. I really enjoyed meeting you though."

No way, it couldn't end like this! I just spent the past two hours being interesting and charming—why was he extending his hand to say good-bye? I had to act quickly or the day's mission would be a complete failure.

"It was really nice meeting you too. Do you want to exchange phone numbers? Maybe we can grab a coffee one afternoon."

"Sure, that would be great."

We gave each other our phone numbers and said good-bye—for the time being.

As he walked away I thought, *I wonder what he looks like with his clothes off.* I was basking in the glow of my delightful afternoon and was caught off guard once again by the women who attacked en masse with noogies and strangleholds. We collapsed into a heap laughing. They teased me about how I had been staring at Roman nonstop. Klara announced that I looked like a fifteen-year-old girl who just had her first conversation with a cute boy. I chased her into the metro station, but I was no match for her long hockey-player strides.

"Do you think he's going to call?" I asked Juliet.

"I don't know, if he doesn't call you have his number—call him."

"I want him to call me. I walked up to him, I asked for his number, I don't want to be the one to call. I want to be the prey not the hunter."

Juliet smiled and rolled her eyes.

"No you don't; you want to get some."

"Good point. . . if I don't hear from him by Wednesday I'll call."

We were sitting on an old barge that had been turned into a bar, having a drink and enjoying the sunset. I heard the text message sound, so I reached into my pocket and pulled out my phone. As I read the message, a huge grin spread across my face.

I HAD A REALLY NICE TIME AT THE RALLY TODAY, BUT THE BEST PART WAS MEETING YOU. I'LL CALL YOU TOMORROW AND WE CAN MAKE PLANS TOGETHER. YOU HAVE BEAUTIFUL EYES BY THE WAY.

I jumped up, threw my hands in the air, and screamed. Looking back it was probably not the butchest possible reaction.

"Juliet, read this," I said. She read the text message aloud since my screeching drew everyone's attention.

"I certainly know the answer to your question now."

Beer glasses were raised as the girls congratulated me on my conquest.

* * * *

I stood in front of the horse statue at the top of Wenceslas Square, the most popular meeting spot in town, waiting for Roman. He arrived ten minutes late. I didn't care, he was here.

He looked even better than he did the day I met him. Wearing crisp new khakis, a blue dress shirt, and a yellow sweater, he was sexy in business casual wear, which is not something everyone can pull off. As he walked toward me I noticed I was a little nervous.

"Hello Marc, sorry I'm late. I hope you weren't waiting too long."

"No I just got here a few minutes ago."

"So, how do you like living in Prague?"

"What's not to like? It's an incredible city," I replied.

"And what about Czech people—do you like them?"

"The ones I've met have been great."

"You don't find them a little negative and depressing?" Roman asked.

Now that he mentioned it, as a group Czechs were not the most cheerful of people. I suppose forty years of communism would put anyone in a bad mood. I didn't think I should say this on our first date though.

"No not at all. I think they're a little more serious than my American friends, but most Czech people are really nice."

This statement was true with several notable exceptions. The old babushkas in the shops—scary and mean as junkyard dogs! One was Olga the pharmacist near where I lived. I'm pretty sure if the devil was a Czech woman the job would be hers. Then there was Smelly Jidka from school who was quite possibly the rudest woman on Earth. She was about seventy, a leftover bureaucrat from the old days. Everyone assumed that she gave up showering thirteen years ago to protest the communists losing power.

"What would you like to do?" Roman asked.

"Why don't we go for a walk around the city and you can show me your favorite spots?"

It was seven o'clock and the sun had just set. Every building was illuminated to perfection and the city had a magnificent glow to it. It was the most romantic setting possible for a first date. Here I was in the land of Kafka, Dvorak, and Havel wandering through the cobblestone streets of old Prague—could this date get any better? As matter of fact, it could. We were looking in a shop window when Roman turned to me and asked, "Would it be alright if I kissed you?"

"I suppose so," I said with a sarcastic grin.

Now not to sound goofy, but as we kissed under the lamplight I was sure imaginary fireworks were going off in my head and my knees literally went weak. He was strong and handsome. I put my arms around him and for the first time felt his enormous shoulders. That wasn't the only thing I felt, I knew if this went on much longer we wouldn't be walking anywhere for quite some time.

"Wow," was the first word that came out of my mouth.

"I don't know that word," Roman said, "but it sounds about right."

"Should we try a second kiss and look for a word that you do know?" I asked Roman.

"No, I want to keep our first kiss in my mind a little while longer. I'm sure there will be many more, but there's only ever one first kiss."

I didn't want this night to end. We spent the rest of the evening hand in hand walking through the city laughing, talking, and enjoying each other's company. I noticed how different it was in Prague; no one really paid much attention to two men walking through the streets holding hands. I love Europe!

A few hours later we arrived at my tram stop.

"I had a really great time tonight," Roman said.

"Me too."

The tram came rumbling up the street.

"I'll talk to you soon Marc."

"You definitely will."

I sat on the tram enjoying that tingly feeling you have right after a night like the one I had had comes to an end. My mobile phone beeped a few minutes later. The text message read "Thank you for a really special night" I stared out the window smiling to myself. I had found my Czech boyfriend—or so I thought.

\* \* \* \*

Roman and I spent a lot of time together over the next several months. In so many ways we had become really close. He was a good person, he was never loud or rude, he was always considerate and attentive—all qualities that shouldn't be taken for granted. So why did I have this nagging feeling that something wasn't quite right?

There were definitely elements to the relationship that were lacking, but whose relationship is perfect? I think the hardest part for me was dealing with the cultural divide. I'm a very pop-culture-oriented person, and being able to make amusing pop-culture references is really important to me. It may sound trivial, but when you're walking through the streets of Prague and see a girl wearing denim shorts that are wedged into her butt crack and yell, "Wow! Those are some serious Daisy Dukes. She's got it going on!" and the only reaction you get is a blank stare, it kind of kills the moment. Or when something happens that you don't like and you look at your boyfriend and say "gggrrrrrrr aarrgggghhhh," which of course is the sound that the Mutant Enemy monster makes as he bounces across the screen during the end credits of the television show *Buffy the Vampire Slayer,* looking at you like you just stole his wallet, and once again your comment lands with a deafening thud. Cultural references are a lot like jokes: they aren't funny if you have to explain them.

Then there was the sex—that translated perfectly, and sex with Roman was amazing. He was exceptionally well built and had huge hands and feet if you know what I mean. Every time he arrived at my apartment I practically ripped his clothes off before he even walked in the door, not that he needed much encouragement mind you. A little while into the relationship I started to wonder why he had never invited me to his apartment. Why were we always at my place?

It turned out Roman was currently residing at his parent's house. About a year before he had broken up with his previous American boyfriend with whom he had been living for seven years. Jim (that was his name) came home one day and announced to Roman that he was going to marry his friend Pria, an Indian ex-nun. It's not the kind of news a gay man could ever really be prepared for. Come to think of it, it's not really the kind of news anyone could be prepared for. *What is the proper response to a statement like that?* I wondered as Roman filled me in on the details of his and Jim's final days. He was understandably devastated by the situation. After learning this fact about him I had a much better sense of why he had been keeping a little distance between us. Roman was obviously afraid of getting hurt again.

A few days after he told me about Jim's shocking revelation, we were arguing. Roman said he knew that one day I would leave Prague. He asked me if I could promise that I wouldn't ever leave the Czech Republic and that we would always be together. Before I could stop myself I blurted out: "No, but I can promise I won't ever marry an Indian ex-nun."

He didn't find my wisecrack amusing at all. He found it even less amusing when he noticed the little smirk on my face. Come on, how often do I get to use a line like that?

* * * *

It was Christmastime and Roman had not told his parents about us, therefore he had no excuse not to spend the holiday with them. I was determined however to have my Czech Christmas with my Czech boyfriend in my Czech apartment and we were going to open Czech presents!

Our celebration took place the week before Christmas.

"Open that one."

"What is it?" Roman asked.

"Well, why you don't open it and find out?" I said with a smile as I bent over and kissed him.

"It's the poster I saw at the national museum that I really liked. You remembered."

"Yes, I did. It's a boyfriend's job to remember things like that."

"Thank you," Roman said.

"It'll look great when you move into your own place."

Right after I said it I knew I shouldn't have brought the subject up again.

"Why are you always doing that? You're always making comments about me moving into my own apartment. When I'm ready I'll move."

I felt his annoyance, and it wasn't the first time either. I didn't want to admit it, but we were drifting apart. I was trying to hold on to something that I knew sooner or later would slip away. Even as we sat exchanging gifts under the Christmas tree we bought and decorated together, I knew his heart wasn't in it. The truth was, this relationship wasn't working and we both knew it. Roman had even steered the conversation toward breaking up once, but I convinced him that there was good stuff here and we should give it some more time. On a separate occasion I initiated the breakup conversation, to which he responded by taking his clothes off. That took the wind out of my sails.

"What time are you leaving tomorrow Marc?"·

"My train is at seven, so I guess I'll leave here around six," I replied. "Do you want to spend the night?"

"No, I should go home; you need your sleep, you have a long trip ahead of you."

It's not a really good sign when you're leaving for ten days and your boyfriend doesn't want to spend the night at your apartment.

I walked Roman to the door.

"You're going to pick me up at the train station on the thirtieth, right?"

"I'll be there," he said with a little smile.

"Don't forget Sarah and Paula are coming from London for New Year's with some of their friends. Daniel is joining us too if that's okay?"

"Of course—we couldn't have a celebration without Daniel could we?"

"Roman, don't be like that."

"Well sometimes I think you'd rather be with him."

"Daniel and I are just friends."

"Are you?" Roman asked.

"You know I would never do that to you."

"I know—I'm sorry," Roman said as he hugged me.

"We can't leave each other being mad, it's not very Christmassy," I said, forcing another unconvincing smile.

"No, we can't," he smiled back.

Roman put on his shoes. We kissed at the door.

"I'll see you at the station on the thirtieth."

"Good night."

"Hey," I yelled into the hallway. Roman popped his head out the elevator. "Merry Christmas."

"You too Marc. Have a great trip."

I walked back into the living room and looked down at the presents. I didn't know if I would have a boyfriend next Christmas or not, but either way I was fairly certain it wouldn't be the one I had now. It made me sad.

\* \* \* \*

The train pulled into Hlavni Nadrazi (Central Station), right on time. My trip to Croatia had been amazing. I walked through the station looking for Roman. Better check my phone, I thought. Sure enough that oh so familiar text message appeared:

I AM SORRY. I WILL BE A LITTLE LATE.

It didn't bother me; I was in a really great mood. My favorite all-female couple was in town, I had booked a table at a fabulous restaurant for New Year's Eve, and I was determined to try and put this relationship back on track. I looked up and there was Roman coming toward me. I gave him a big hug. I could tell he was uncomfortable.

"How was Christmas in Croatia?" He asked.

"It was great!" Christmas in Croatia—it made me laugh every time I heard it. "It sounds like a Bob Hope special. 'Ladies and gentlemen, welcome to Christmas in Croatia,'" I said to Roman.

"Who's Bob Hope?"

"Who's Bob Hope?" I asked with a slightly annoyed look on my face. I decided to just let it go.

"Come on tall handsome Czech boy, let's go back to my house so we can say hello to each other properly." I put my hand on Roman's shoulder. More discomfort.

On the way home he asked about my trip. I asked him how his Christmas was. It was all terribly polite—not a conversation that boyfriends who had been apart for almost two weeks should be having. We got off the tram and Roman stopped on the corner of my street.

"I'm not coming up," he said.

"What do you mean you're not coming up?" I fired back angrily.

"We have to talk."

. No, we didn't, because it was very clear what the conversation was going to be about and I really didn't want to have it.

"You're breaking up with me the night before New Year's? You asshole!"

I took a moment to regroup. If this was it, I wanted to have farewell sex at least. I obviously wasn't thinking clearly. It must have been a combination of two weeks without any and travel fatigue.

"Fine, whatever Roman, just come upstairs and spend the night. We can talk in the morning."

I figured once I had him upstairs he would forget about this ridiculous notion of breaking up right before New Year's. We would break up when I was ready. And did I mention that I really really wanted to have sex? He was not cooperating with my plan at all.

"I think we should break up," Roman declared.

"Wow, you know what? You're really being a dick." Even my insults sometimes got lost in the cultural black hole. "What a nice welcome-home conversation Roman."

"I'm so sorry Marc, this is really hard for me too, but I've had a lot of time to think about us while you were away. I can't just come up and spend the night like everything's fine when I know it isn't."

"Oh goody for you Roman, Mr. Fucking Boo Hoo This Is So Hard for Me Too but I'm So Mature and I'm Going to Be an Adult About It—fuck you! Roman, I'm so over you right now. I'm tired and I need to go upstairs." I turned and started to walk away.

"I'll call you tomorrow," Roman yelled after me as I marched off.

"Yeah, blow me, whatever," I said as I threw my hand in the air. I'm sure I even had a little head bob going on.

I got upstairs and thought about what just happened. I suppose I could have handled it a little better, but I was angry and tired. I was also really upset for several reasons. First of all, now I was going to be the tragic figure on New Year's Eve without a boyfriend who just got dumped. Second of all, I knew this was coming to an end, but I really wanted a few more weeks of good sex. Third of all, he beat me to it. When the time came I wanted to break up with him. There was only one thing I could think of that would make me feel better—cookies, and lots of them.

After a dozen or so Oreos and a half gallon of milk, as I had suspected I would I did indeed feel much better. I've always believed in the magical healing power of chocolate. I needed to call Paula and Sarah at their hotel to make sure they arrived safely. I told them I was exhausted from my trip, but I would meet them for brunch tomorrow. They were so excited to meet Roman. I didn't have the energy to tell them. I got into bed and punched my pillow. I punched it a little harder and imagined it was Roman's face. A few more punches and the combination of anger release, cookie digestion, and tryptophan got the better of me, and I nodded off.

\* \* \* \*

I walked into the Four Seasons Hotel the next morning to find Paula and Sarah sharing a bottle of champagne, laughing and fooling around as usual.

"What are you two, like, drinking at eleven in the morning? Ya lesbian lushes." I jumped on them and we all sank into the couch.

"I'm on holiday, I can drink as much as I want," Sarah replied as she greeted me with her trademark toothy grin.

"Hello darling," Paula said. "How are you?"

"I'm fine girls," I hugged them both and started to sob.

"Oh that's not good," Paula said.

I filled them in on the details of the past several months including previous night's events.

"What a wanker," Sarah said when I was finished.

"He's obviously a complete tosser," was Paula's reply.

"Don't worry sweetie, I'll make Sarah beat him up for you."

There is no question that Sarah is a formidable woman, and a fight between her and Roman actually might have been interesting.

"No, thank you, I appreciate the offer though. He really is a good guy—the whole thing has just gone 'tits up' as you would say."

My mobile phone rang. It was Roman.

"It's him—I'll be back."

Roman and I had a very civilized conversation. We talked about what happened the night before and made our amends to one another. I walked back to the couch where Sarah and Paula were sitting to fill them in on the details of the chat we just had.

"Okay, here's the deal. I don't want there to be any unnecessary drama tonight, so this is what's going to happen: Roman is still coming to dinner but you two are the only ones who are going to know about us breaking up. We both agreed that there's no reason to make everyone feel uncomfortable.

"Are you sure you're okay with that darling?" Paula asked.

"We'll find out soon enough, won't we?"

"Well, you don't need to decide now, but the offer for Sarah to beat him up is still stands."

Sarah jumped off the couch, flexed, and tried to look menacing, which of course made us laugh.

* * * *

Kampa Park is one of the best restaurants in Prague and a perfect setting for a romantic New Year's Eve dinner—unless you have just been dumped by your boyfriend, then it's nothing more than an overpriced tourist trap with tiny little portions and stinky candles everywhere. We had a reservation for ten, in addition to Sarah and Paula, Roman and myself, there were two other couples from London, Daniel, and Martin, Roman's friend. I doubt anyone noticed anything was different between Roman and me, except the ever-perceptive Daniel.

"Are you and Roman mad at each other?"

"No, why?"

"It just seems like something is wrong. Is it?"

Not wanting to lie, I told Daniel the truth, but explained I didn't want to make a big deal about it tonight. Who knew how many New Year's Eve's I would spend in Prague, and I just wanted to enjoy myself. Everyone ate, laughed, drank, wore silly hats and behaved the way people should behave on New Year's Eve. It really was a nice dinner. Roman and I sat next to each other, but spent most of the night talking to other people.

We left the restaurant around 11:30 and found a good spot alongside the river. Thousands of people had gathered to watch the fireworks over Prague Castle. Roman and I exchanged glances, I'm sure we were both thinking about how many late-night walks we had taken together through the winding streets around the castle.

"How you holding up love?" Paula asked.

"I'm fine. I'm glad you and Sarah are here."

"So are we."

"Roman's lovely," Paula said.

"No he's not—he's a pig who dumped your friend yesterday, remember?"

"Yes darling, but aside from that he's lovely."

"I know, that's what makes this even worse—he's such a nice person and all my friends really like him."

Paula and I looked over at Sarah who was chasing one of her friends, trying to poke her in the ass with a sparkler.

I had been avoiding Roman a good part of the evening. As it drew closer to midnight the couples started recoupling.

"Are you having fun?" he asked.

"Yeah, you?"

"Yes, your friends are very nice."

"Thanks they really like you too—of course they don't know how evil you are for what you did to me."

"My timing was bad," he said.

"Ya think so?"

"You know it was the right thing to do Marc, even if it wasn't the right time to do it."

"I know Roman, but it really sucks. You're a great guy and we had a lot of fun together. It's just sad that it's over."

"Marc, I know I've said this before, it wasn't an easy decision for me either. I think you're adorable and smart and you're someone who I trust. Do you think it's easy to walk away from that? We had some really incredible times, but we're just too different to make this work."

"I know you're right," I said with a sigh of reluctant acceptance. "Hey Roman."

"Yeah?"

"Can we still have New Year's Eve sex? Bar's closing, last call, one for the road so to speak," I said with a smile.

Roman smiled back. "That sounds like a good way to end it to me."

This time the fireworks were very real, different from the imaginary fireworks I saw that night on our first date a few months before. It's amazing how relationships evolve over such a short period of time. You meet someone who is a complete stranger, you spend more time with them than with anyone else in your life even though a little while ago you didn't even know they existed, you trust them with your most intimate secrets, and then as quickly as they entered your life, they're gone.

Everyone was staring into the night sky watching the fireworks light up the city. It was a beautiful sight. The year 2002 was officially here. Roman took my hand in his. He and I were not to be, but as the saying goes, it was great while it lasted. Six months later I did indeed leave Prague as Roman had predicted. I looked over at Sarah and Paula who were locked in an embrace and thought, that's what real love looks like. Sarah saw me getting a little teary and whispered something in Paula's ear.

"Happy New Year Roman."

"Happy New Year Marc."

We hugged each other. It was a different kind of hug than we were used to. It was a hug two people share who know what they had was almost over. It was a hug that said "I don't want to let you go and I'll miss you." It was one of those hugs where you squeeze a little harder and hold on a little longer. When we finally did let go, we looked at each other as if to say, everything would be okay, in time.

Somehow friends always seem to know how to prevent things from getting too serious and when to put the celebration back on track. Sarah and Paula ran over, knocked me to the ground, and smothered me with New Year's Eve kisses.

What is it about lesbians and their obsession with tackling people?

# ଈ 2

# My Canterbury Tale
# or the House in Broadstairs

*Michael T. Luongo*

It was the closest in my life that I ever came to being kept. I don't look on this period with a sense of shame, but rather with confusion, confusion about where I was in life at the time of the relationship, coupled with an intense loneliness I felt living in rural England.

Nathan and I met in Holborn station on the London Underground, the stop made famous in the scene from the movie *Secrets and Lies*. That this would be where we had the first encounter that gave birth to our strange and twisted relationship was absolutely appropriate, for I became the secret that helped to maintain his lie.

I was with my best friends in London—Ian, David, and Veronique, the latter two a mixed British and French couple. We were headed out to meet some other friends, one of whom, Rachel, Ian had hoped to date. Nathan was her older brother. The evening out was meant to be an occasion for Rachel and shy Ian to see how things might work out, within the comfort of a group of friends. I was just along for the ride.

The moment I saw Nathan, something about him struck me. I distinctly remember passing through the turnstiles at the station, coming across him in his leather jacket, an umbrella in his hand. He and Rachel along with several other friends had been waiting for us to arrive. He was handsome, with unruly, thick black hair. He looked a little like John Kennedy Jr. I knew immediately that I would have sex with him that night. It was a feeling that I had, and in that time, at that age, in my late twenties, it was quite common, and perhaps its own self-fulfilling prophecy.

*Looking for Love in Faraway Places*
© 2007 The Haworth Press, Inc. All rights reserved.
doi:10.1300/5366_02

I cannot remember exactly where we were headed, but somewhere we had reservations at a restaurant that could hold us all. We were in a large group, nearly ten of us, a noisy bunch breaking into little cliques as we made our way through the rainy and crowded London streets. When we finally arrived at the restaurant, I made sure that I seated myself next to Nathan. I had to interact with him, I knew I could make some sort of a connection, even if he did mention a girlfriend somewhere along the walk to the restaurant.

My being gay was never a secret, and came up in conversation casually with everyone else. I had known my London friends since my college backpacking days, and in spite of their living on another continent, I considered them to be among my very closest. Nathan seemed fascinated by my candor on the subject, claiming he had never met someone openly gay. In London in 1997 I found this virtually impossible to believe, but then perhaps it all depends on one's circles.

I was in graduate school at the time, pursuing a master's degree in urban planning at Rutgers University. My current project was on the globalization of dance music, comparing the club scenes of New York and London and looking at their geographic distribution within the cities. I often chose odd topics, even if they meant that professors would roll their eyes in disbelief at my presentations, stretching the limits of what they might have considered legitimate research. This was the time when New York's fascistic Mayor Giuliani, who took delight in closing down dance clubs, was wreaking havoc on New York nightlife. London was fun to go out in; New York had become hit or miss.

I told Nathan some of the clubs I had planned to visit that night, none of which were gay. SW1, the Velvet Underground, and many others were on the list. He explained to me his past love of clubbing, and his sister Rachel chimed in about what a partier he once was. Nathan proposed to come along with me. It had been ages he said since he had gone out. He wanted to help me, he explained, be my escort out in his town. Fortunately, no one else of the large group wanted to join us. I wanted time alone with him to see where the night might lead us.

We went from club to club, the rain doing nothing to get in our way. Nathan knew the scene well, picking each place by the style of music—techno, electronica, trance, ambient. I don't remember how many clubs we went to that night, but Nathan paid for the expensive admission in every single one, buying me drinks along the way. We stayed and danced together for awhile in one where a man banged drums on the dance floor, mirroring the rhythms of the turntables. We might have been in the club for an hour, but the drummer never stopped, perhaps fueled by meth, and his face was locked in a trance, the crowds staring at him in awe.

I loved music and dancing, and music and dancing only, but Nathan added a third element: he loved drugs too. Clubs had meant that to him, whether it was coke, or crystal or ecstasy, and he found it hard to step into one without partaking of something. In fact, he explained that that was why he gave it up all together and had not been out for a few years. I liked that he was telling me this, that he could confide in me. His own sister didn't know of his drug problem, even though he thought of their relationship as close. Music alone to me was drug enough when I went dancing. I never understood why others needed anything more. Dancing, however, always led to my one true vice— sex with people who were only recently before strangers. I still continued to hope that would be the case, but as night wore on, I found so many conflicting clues about Nathan's sexuality. Finally, sunlight began to hit the edge of the city. Nathan asked me to come home with him, to his apartment in the western suburbs of London.

When we arrived, I still wasn't completely sure where I stood with him, but once we entered the house I had a much better idea. I remember three photos of flowers on the wall above his stereo system, each in black frames. They were exquisite and hung in perfect balance. They were nothing a straight man would have ever picked out for decorating. The rest of the house was equally tasteful and immaculate. Sure, there are anally retentive straight metrosexuals, but this went far beyond that. I asked if he had hired someone to decorate. He told me had done everything himself, making me smirk inside.

He showed me his enormous CD collection, playing some of the music we'd heard in the clubs. He promised he would make me tapes of what I liked and send them to me in America with a letter. I began to tease him at this point, telling him I didn't know of too many men who write each other letters, unless their interests lie in other things. He was taken aback, and I argued with him that I thought that he might be gay but was too afraid to admit it. I pointed at the pictures above the stereo as justification, but he saw nothing gay about the ability to decorate with style.

But that was when he admitted to his curiosity, and to why he had decided to go out through the night with me and finally bring me home. He mentioned again that I was the first gay person he had ever known. Now, seeing that he lived in the suburbs and not Central London, I thought perhaps that could be correct.

We moved from the living room into the bedroom, and for someone who claimed to have never been with a man, Nathan seemed to know what he was doing. Perhaps it was all a continuation of lie, a projection to make himself feel better about his thoughts. But then again, even when it truly was my first time, I wasn't awkward. When there is something you long to do all your life, there is no way you can mess it up when the opportunity finally arises.

The next morning Nathan dropped me off at Veronique and David's home. He swore me to secrecy, but when Veronique asked, "He's a homo, isn't he?" I told her everything. Yet months later on a phone call when the subject came up I denied to her anything had ever happened, that I had made it all up that morning to impress her. Somehow, I guiltily thought, I had to protect Nathan's secret. I was a connection to this world he wanted to enter but was far too afraid to.

This was because once I had returned to the United States I had kept in touch with Nathan through letters and phone calls. Somehow, I felt he could be a project of mine. Maybe I could help him find himself, allow him to come out without fear. With each letter, as he had promised, Nathan sent the music tapes he made from his CD collection. He wrote in the letters that he would lie on his couch thinking of me as he listened to the music he was recording, remembering the night that we'd met. I looked forward to the tapes and I'd blast them in my car and put myself into a trance, perhaps most dangerously when I rode through the Holland and Lincoln tunnels late at night, at high speeds, ignoring everything around me. The rhythms, mixed with the lights of cars bulleting around me in those tiled tubes were like musical ecstasy.

By the end of that year, close to the time I was finishing all the credit requirements for my master's, I was offered a research job in Canterbury, England, in what had to be one of the happiest e-mails in my life. The position was at Canterbury Christ Church College, the teaching institution of the Church of England, now part of the University of Kent. The job was something I was perfect for—looking at HIV prevention in the context of travel as special advisors to THT, the Terrence Higgins Trust, the United Kingdom's main HIV organization. My boss Samuel was a professor I'd met about two years before, after discovering each other's research. I had asked him long before for a job, feeling out of place in doing so, but now here I was, his research assistant. In theory, I was doing sex research for the Church of England, and therefore, indirectly, I was in service to Her Majesty, the Queen herself. It was something I could not pass up.

Reality sunk in once the job had started. I had an exceedingly interesting job that paid exceedingly little. This was bad enough in New York, and so much worse in shockingly expensive England. Still the job meant travel, and I would be doing research all over England and at gay resorts in the Mediterranean, but this was tempered by the physical setting of where I would be based. To go from working in Manhattan to a tiny Elizabethan town of half-timbered houses that could double as a stage for a Shakespeare play was a tremendous cultural shock. I went from big, bold, and brassy to a quiet reserved office. I worried incessantly that I might be too pushy for the place, and I always tried to keep that in check. To be sure, the town of Canterbury was beautiful, but there was nothing to do there. Other than the people in my office, with whom I was very close, it was difficult to make friends with the reserved residents. I remember when I had first met Samuel, and as the train pulled out of Canterbury giving way to miles of fields and hills on its return to London I had thought of how desolate it seemed, how lonely and remote a place for a gay man to live. I found out soon enough how true those thoughts had been.

For my apartment, I wound up living in Margate several miles away, a Georgian-era town on the North Sea, not too far from Dover. Its glory days had long passed, and now it was desolate and forlorn. My landlord Patrick was a friend of Samuel's, and he had just bought an enormous old house that was once a Victorian hotel. Eventually, when the town's resort days ended, the hotel became a down-on-its-luck halfway house for drug addicts, and it was now a messy shell of a building in desperate need of overhaul as the neighborhood began to gentrify.

Still, there was something about the area that reminded me of childhood. I grew up in Springsteen country, the fabled Jersey Shore. My home was slightly inland in the new and comfortable suburbs, but only a few minutes away were the shattered 1920's resorts like Asbury Park, their empty hotels and casinos sea-worn ruins filled with nesting seagulls and the homeless when I was growing up, gloriously desolate witnesses to an era when time in the sun was a train ride not a plane ride away from Manhattan. Margate was the same, full of old hotels, many of which, like the one I was living in, once housed the homeless, the down on their luck, the people no one wanted. But the sea was forever, never caring about the manmade structures that rested on its beaches. Its eternity, like the shore I grew up on, remained a solace to walk along and look out onto. London was still so very close, even if its busy pace and grandeur seemed a psychological eternity from Margate, as Manhattan does from Asbury Park. In so many ways Margate was like home, like childhood. I could get used to being here, even if vague dissatisfaction and a longing to be at the center of things permeated my being, as it did my whole life before my own move from the suburbs into Manhattan.

My saving grace, however, was Nathan. Small world that it was, he owned a vacation home the next town over from Margate, in Broadstairs, near the famous Bleak House immortalized by Charles Dickens. It became our little love hideaway, a place where we could continue our secret relationship, away from the eyes of our mutual friends in London. It was virtually my first weekend there that Nathan came to visit, and he whisked me away to the house. The bookshelves were full of decorating magazines, and the décor was a pure and radiant white. Driftwood sat carefully posed in the corners of the house, elements of the nearby seaside brought indoors. Like his house in London, it was Nathan who had done all of the decorating on his own.

Periodically I had to be in London for meetings with the Terrence Higgins Trust. I usually scheduled these for Fridays so that I could have the whole weekend in town. If I was not meeting Ian or David or Veronique I met with Nathan. It became odd explaining gaps in my time in London to my friends, as if I were having an affair of some sort against them, cheating on them, trying to squeeze in moments with Nathan whenever possible. And yet, I was not the one with a secret. He was.

Nathan took me to fancy restaurants, the latest trendiest places in London that I could never dare think of to afford. The bill was always left to him, in credit cards, or big flashy 100 pound notes, the heavy gold bracelet on his hairy wrist catching the table's candlelight as he handed the payments to the waiter.

Nathan seemed to relish the thought of spending money on me, though none of the things were ever anything permanent like clothes or jewelry. It was his way of taking care of me, as much as I felt I was taking care of him too, trying to make him comfortable in his sexuality. But with each meal paid for, I felt like less and less of a person, with less control of my part of the relationship.

He had even given me a cell phone, a relative luxury at that time. Ostensibly it was so he could reach me whenever he wanted. One day I used it recklessly, making an expensive call to a friend back home in the United States. Nathan got the bill and admonished me, and I felt like a child being reprimanded by his father.

For someone my age, Nathan was a very successful businessman. He had a lot of money and liked to show it, an ostentation not always in line with a British mentality. His car was a convertible, a useless item in London, but when he visited me in Margate we would put the top down, tooling along the roads of the North Sea as if they were the Pacific Coast Highway.

Eventually, Nathan granted me full-time use of his Broadstairs house in addition to our little weekend trysts. I loved being in the town because I felt it put me close to Dickens. I thought somehow there was something special here, something that I as a writer hoped to become a part of. Bleak House was now a museum, and I would go there to touch Dickens's desk in a room with a view to the North Sea, thinking that perhaps I could absorb some of its energy, absorb some of his writing power.

I began to live in Broadstairs more than at my own place in Margate. Most of all, his house was a retreat from my manic-depressive landlord Patrick who would in the course of an hour go from a funny drag comedy act to arguing violently with his lover Joseph. Their dog, a messy incontinent puppy, was like their child, and featured often in their arguments. If I did not take Patrick's side there was always the chance I'd be thrown out of the house, like his lover often was, even though he was usually the one in the right. Patrick was insatiably cruel at times. He was a professor at Canterbury Christ Church College, and he often put down Joseph for being uneducated. Why they stayed together, I had no idea. My work transcribing interviews, locked away in my room, earphones on in front of my computer was my only escape, until Nathan gave me those keys to his house.

Perhaps the spirit of Dickens did haunt the town, because I did some of my best writing in that house. Alone in the darkness of the evening I had no distractions, only a crackling fire next to me and my laptop. At night, when I was restless, or had woken up after accidentally falling asleep on the couch as I wrote my master's thesis or reports from work, I would slip outside and head toward the dark waterfront. Here, seagulls screamed overhead, and the fog shimmied in over old wooden fishing boats rocking in the rough North Sea. It was quintessential England, a step back to the very time of Dickens, a lonely haunting vista unchanged for 150 years.

The weekends, though, were for Nathan. I began to take fewer trips into London as our relationship progressed, letting a little part of what I wanted to do succumb to his will. I felt so much more free in London, away from the confines of rural England. And my friends were all there. But Nathan felt so much more free visiting me here, away from any possibility of ever running into people he knew and having to explain me to them.

Nathan usually was the one to initiate sex, but it was I who took control in bed, still playing teacher to him. Late at night when we were fooling around, I would finger him, hoping to condition him for anal sex if it ever came to that between us. It was fascinating to watch his face as I entered him, trying to make him feel comfortable with what a man who says he was not gay should consider a violation. But even if in bed I took the lead, it became increasingly harder for me to say no to him when it came to sex. After all, he was sort of keeping me. I wondered at the time if this is what some women go through. It's good perhaps for men to be in such a situation, if only simply to see how women who were or are totally dependant on their husband's income might have to live, placed in a position by society to be the ones taken care of, even in this day and age. Yet, even while I enjoyed it in many ways, and Nathan saved me from the loneliness I was experiencing in isolated rural England, I always somehow felt like less because of it. Here I was examining the sexual lives of other men for work, yet ashamed and unable to confront the problems and insecurities that existed in my own. Who was I to judge and write on others, when I barely could even grasp the odd framework of the relationship I was in? Still, with our relationship as undefined as his sexuality, Nathan and I had no pretense of fidelity toward each other. In fact, after we would have sex, he often asked me about all the other men I had slept with while I was living there in England. It was a long list.

My job took me all over country, testing project material in focus groups of young men recruited at various HIV-prevention organizations. At night though, my time was my own, and I would use it to check out the local gay scene in whatever town I happened to find myself. I would tell Nathan stories of the men I would meet, like Paul, a man infamous for the largest balls in Bristol, who explained how everyone gasped when they pulled down his pants in bed. I was certainly in that category of encounters for him. Or the corner room in the New Union Pub Hotel in Manchester, overlooking a notorious cruising site where I would look out the window, luring men up one at a time, every half-hour, until I exhausted myself.

"You slut," Nathan would sometimes say to me in feigned shock after I recounted my stories. But it was also I think a way to make himself feel better about what he had just done in bed with me, a form of projection. Still, why I let myself be told these things, even if they were in jest, would get to me. Perhaps I deserved some form of mental cruelty for being kept by him. What of his own untruth, simply being here in bed with me was one of those, yet he still chose to cast stones. In the end, though, I think my ability to move from bed to bed, and be open in my sexuality, is what intrigued him most about me from that first night we met.

One morning, as we laid in the white folds of the bed, the room purified by the intense light it received through the window, Nathan decided to tell me that he had developed a relationship with a man at work, one of his employees, who was married and had a baby. Like the relationship he had with me, there was something wrong with it. They never had sex, though there was always the hint that it might happen. After work they would go out drinking, the young man sometimes crying drunk in Nathan's arms about how much he loved him, never mentioning the word gay or where the feelings came from. This had gone on for many months, and Nathan's only reply to him was that he had a wife and child, and should stop living a lie, and admit to himself that he was gay. The young man worried about losing his friends, losing his family. "He tells me he loves me, but as a buddy. I tell him it is something deeper," Nathan told me. He never was able to understand the irony of his own advice.

Eventually, after many months, it came time for me to leave England. The funding for the travel and HIV project had run out, and I could return home in time to walk at my master's graduation ceremony. I stayed late in the office my last night, my workaholic American tendencies getting the best of me. I wanted to make sure that all the loose ends were tied, though I am sure that Samuel would not have minded if there were some things left undone. Patrick kept calling me in the office, imploring me to come home to Margate right away. When I finally did, he made me cry. He had been planning a surprise party for me, complete with an Asian drag show. I knew this only because when he opened the door for me he was wearing his fake white fur coat with the panda printed on the back, the most over-the-top and ridiculous thing you can imagine. When he wandered the house with it, it signaled he was in the mood to perform a show and you had to stop whatever you were doing or feel his wrath. Joseph was at the table sitting over a smashed cake, saying nothing. They must have had some horrible argument about the surprise going away party for me that I had ruined inadvertently. My final night with them was spent being told by Patrick how terrible a tenant and friend I was, while I tried to pack things for my flight the next day.

Nathan drove from London to take me to the airport. Tremendously out of his way since he lived near it, but he wanted to make sure to see me before I left. I don't remember when my flight was, but we had plenty of time that day. We made a stop at the house in Broadstairs, ostensibly to pick up something that he needed in London, but it was really so we could have sex one last time. As we lay in bed after cuddling for a few brief moments, I looked around the room for the last time, taking in its radiant whiteness. Were it not for the house, and for Nathan, and for our secret sessions, I might never have made it through my time here in lonely rural England. Nathan and I still remained in touch through phone calls and the letters he would continue to send with music tapes. This lasted for nearly a year, but then suddenly ended. For a long time I heard nothing more from him except for Christmas cards once a year.

Then, 9/11 happened. I was barraged by calls at that time from people checking in on me. Even one-night stands from all over the world who somehow still had my number wanted desperately to make sure I was alive. Nathan called me on my cell phone when I was walking around my neighborhood. I was doing the most mundane thing imaginable after the tragedy—grocery shopping, with the added twist of chatting with people on the street whom I saw everyday but never bothered to get to know until then.

Once Nathan knew that I was okay, he degenerated into the conversation we once had in England, about the employee whom he thought was gay, the one who would cry in his arms when they were out late together. It seemed that by now the relationship might have been consummated, but Nathan kept that point vague. He instead began a long rant about how the man had to confront his own demons, stop living a lie, and come out to himself and to his family. I was nothing more than a sounding board as he continued for an hour about all the reasons he thought this man was gay and that it was impacting their friendship.

Listening to Nathan talk about this man with whom he was so obviously in love, I wouldn't say that I felt replaced in his affections. I was instead, only disillusioned, disillusioned with what had happened to my project. I listened, perhaps with a hint of judgement. All the things he was saying were advice that perhaps Nathan should have taken for himself, but will never, it seems, be prepared to do. He had never changed, he had never learned, he was as much in denial as the young man he was describing. So many years later and with someone new, he still maintains the secrets that sustain his lies. And I still continue to think of him as my English boyfriend.

# Blue Asia

*Richard D. Thompson*

I lingered in a cool, dark bar, drinking Mekong whiskey to dull out the sense of failure that riddled me this last day in Bangkok. The young waitress sat another drink in front of me, her eye trying to catch mine. I thanked her and glanced away. I'm sure I looked like a potential customer for more than just drinks. I was in my early thirties, athletic, friendly, though distant and desperately horny.

I watched a fly bang its head on the window, again and again, slowly wearing itself out. I stung with feelings I had been able to ignore or suppress while hiking in the jungle mountains near Chiang Mai in the north. There, though content, I had looked forward to being back in a city, where anonymity permits transgression of the social boundaries that keep small-town people separate, prisoners of village gossip. Now, surrounded by millions of Thais in Bangkok, I felt painful hot flashes of desire for the handsome men I saw everywhere.

Before traveling to Asia I had never found East Asians attractive. They were not unattractive, but they had never commanded sexual power over me. Now, after several months of travel in East Asia, I was dumbstruck by the beauty and sexual attraction of Asian men.

I drank more. My desire became more fierce, my heart pounded, and my breathing deepened as I recalled a young Thai man I had seen on a sugar-sanded beach on the island of Koh Samui. He was maybe nineteen, his broad shoulders shirtless and brown. His jet-black hair gleamed in the morning sun, and muscle outlined the nascent form of a grown man. I nodded from afar at the boy, who brooded suspiciously, nodded back, and walked away. I watched him disappear

*Looking for Love in Faraway Places*
© 2007 The Haworth Press, Inc. All rights reserved.
doi:10.1300/5366_03

around the bend as waves erased his tracks from the white sand. I was devastated.

It happened again with a Thai man in his thirties I saw while riding a bus up the Malay Peninsula. He had strong shoulders that tapered down to a lean waist, and his thick thighs filled out his white trousers. Butterflies tickled my stomach every time I looked at him. I recalled chatting with him during a rest stop. I was unnerved by his politeness and graciousness. His manner seemed as beautiful as his body. When the bus arrived in Bangkok, I watched him step off into the arms of a young Thai woman, black hair down to her waist. The two walked away together, hand in hand. It was like death.

A delighted shriek pulled my attention back to the present, to the end of the bar where some men joked and flirted with five or six bare-shouldered Thai women. I envied them. Why couldn't I be straight like them? It must, I liked to imagine, be so much easier.

I left a tip and an untouched drink on the bar and rushed out to escape my memories. I made my way to the Patpong district where red and blue neon signs everywhere invited customers in to enjoy the nightlife. My gaze would often fasten upon handsome men, but their eyes always looked past mine, searching out the women who flirted with them on the street.

My own needy eyes were finally acknowledged by the smile of two Thai men sashaying up the street. Somewhat embarrassed, I walked over to them to bluntly ask which was a club for men.

"Uh...excuse me," I began.

"Boys?" one asked mischievously before I could speak. I just looked at them mutely. They laughed. "BOYS! You want boys?" "Yes," I answered softly. "I want boys."

"You come," one said with a knowing look.

We soon ducked into a dingy tourist shop where they spoke furtively in Thai to a sweaty, rotund little man. He nodded enthusiastically and joined them. He led us through a suffocating, rain-puddled alley with laundry hanging from tiny balconies above, to a corrugated metal warehouse. The man ushered us in with a quiet word to a handsome but surly security guard outside and flicked on an overhead fluorescent light. Swarms of insects clouded the bleached light.

"You wait," said the guard, looking at me with contempt. Meanwhile the little man exited through a small door in the back.

After a tense minute, the little man emerged from the back door with two skinny teenage Thai boys, soft and pasty, with blotched skin. They stood matter of factly for my inspection. The man turned to me with an oily mouth and said, "Boys."

"Good boys," the man said, rubbing his stubby fingers together and smiling. "Very cheap." Repulsed, I nervously circled the boys, as if to appraise them.

When near the door, I said firmly, "No, thank you," and pressed past the guard, out the door into the street. I hurried along the fetid alley fighting the urge to run, listening for them, striding quickly to the nearest big street, afraid the men might come after me for my wallet. They had nothing to lose by robbing me.

Senses sharpened by fear, I found my way back to Patpong. My mouth watered at the smell of curried chicken and grilled seafood in the restaurants. My ears heard every murmur amid the contest of disco music blaring from the bars and the hawkers trying to steer me into strip joints. I gritted my teeth and clinched my fists in frustration.

I suddenly noticed a pair of men going into a windowless bar. Watching the door, I saw several other men enter and leave the club. Relief flooded into me. I knew I had found the right place. I crossed the street and went inside.

It was dark but lively, chattering everywhere. My eyes adjusted to the dimness and I ordered a Mekong whiskey and looked around, feeling the first real pleasure in many days. Thai men, some obviously gay, some not, drank at a polished teak bar. Westerners—Australians, Americans, and Europeans—were also there. All eyes were riveted to a slide show featuring Caucasian men nude or in swimsuits.

Scanning the room, I was thrilled to note a pair of dark eyes fastened on mine. A Thai of thirty or so smiled at me. He had a handsome face on the small-statured Greek body that is prevalent in Thailand—the wide shoulders, narrow hips, and long muscular legs.

I blushed as the man made his way through the crowd and spoke to me. I'd been to gay bars in many countries, but here my heart pounded out of my chest. Desire inflamed me more than any time in my life. The Thais exerted an almost mystical allure. I was hooked.

"You American?" the Thai asked me.

"Yes."

"Oh...I am Thai. My name is Charlie."

"My name is Rick," I said, gratefully shaking his hand. A thrill raced through both my stomach and groin. He smiled with all his might. I wanted to drop to my knees and say, "Thank you! Thank you!" but I held my composure, or thought I did, and smiled back as radiantly as I could muster.

"Rick...hmm," Charlie mulled the name over. "Rick. I like this name."

"Thanks. I like the name Charlie. Uh, how did you *get* the name Charlie?" I wondered how much English Charlie actually spoke.

"My American friend give to me. I like. I keep."

"You keep the American or the name?"

"Both! But name last longer." We laughed.

We immediately liked each other. Charlie spoke broken but comprehensible English and understood most of what I said. This made heat burn inside my chest, and made my hands shake, mouth dry, and my cock hard. My mind and tongue were the only things not thrown into desperate animation.

We chatted a few more minutes and Charlie said, "You strong man. Very okay by me. We go?"

"Yeah. Where?"

"Anywhere!" We laughed again.

"We go!" Charlie said. We walked along the street, where Charlie pointed out various gay bars.

He took me to a simple hotel near Lumpini Park. The ceiling fan creaked softly as we made love all night, stopping only to shower, kiss, and start over again. It was one of those nights that punctuate life with an exclamation mark, one that stands out among the deepest, best spent hours of a lifetime.

Too soon rays of sun streamed through a dark green palm outside the window. The light suffused the room with yellow, setting off the turquoise blue of its walls. I put my lips on Charlie's neck and lay still.

This was a peak of my life; time passed without any thought. I was completely present in the moment. I was free of grief, regret, desire, free of past and future. It was one of the finest hours I've ever lived.

Charlie stretched languidly and opened his eyes.

I smiled. "Good morning."

"Good morning American boy!" Charlie hugged me.

"Want to have breakfast Charlie?" I was happy to be with him, but felt the return of concern, of time's passage, the inevitable loss of an ultimate experience.

Charlie looked down. "You say last night in Bangkok? Now today going Hong Kong!"

"Yeah . . ."

"No! Stay longer."

"My flight is booked. My friend is waiting for me there with his girlfriend."

"No! We stay here another day." Charlie threw his arms around my neck.

"Charlie, I've got to go to Hong Kong...I'm broke here...I've spent all my Thai money because I'm leaving today, and I have to pick up U.S. dollars in Hong Kong to live on."

*Why?* I wondered, *do I always finally meet somebody the night before I, or they, have to go?* It seemed like a law of the universe.

"I get money," Charlie said. "*Please,* you no leave. Stay with me. Why go? We share love. Please stay."

"You can really get some money? I don't know. I don't want to live off of you."

"No matter. No worry! Please stay baby. You good man. First good man in long time. What you have in Hong Kong better than this?"

I picked up the phone and postponed my departure.

\* \* \* \*

Charlie wanted me to meet his friends that afternoon at an apartment on the fifteenth floor of a high-rise building. It was also his plan, only disclosed to me upon our arrival, to win the necessary money by playing cards with them.

"These my friends," Charlie explained as they entered the room. "You welcome too." The room smelled of mint. A fan quietly whirred near the window. Several Thai men in underwear were playing cards in a circle on the floor.

One muscular soldier, his uniform strewn on the floor behind him contemplated his hand as a diminutive queen sat next to him stroking his knee. Two younger men, obviously in love, arms around each other's shoulders, studied their jointly held hand of cards. A good-looking stud, midtwenties, combed his glossy hair at the sink.

Charlie had predicted well. I was very welcome. As Charlie introduced them, each looked me up and down, with undisguised sexual interest and friendly hellos. We joined the card-playing ring. Charlie contributed some cash to the game and drew a hand. As the game wore on, I began to feel ill at ease because they were all obviously discussing me in Thai. They made their thoughts clear by rubbing my shoulders, stroking my knee, and one even reached over and gave my crotch a good squeeze. Although they were benevolent toward me, they seemed to regard me as a toy, and as the card game dragged on my temper rose from so much unwelcome touching and groping. I tried to show nothing. Charlie turned to me.

"They want to know if you are 'king' or 'queen,'" he said proudly. "I tell them, 'king—every time.'" Which was not entirely true. Charlie's high spirits dwindled as the afternoon passed, and he eventually lost the money he had hoped to multiply.

That evening, over a meager dinner, Charlie told me he had been raised in a provincial town near a resort catering to Westerners at the beach resort of Phuket. Charlie had married a local girl, got a job at the resort, and fathered two children. At his job he met an American man who worked at the resort's management firm. Charlie fell completely in love with him. They had an intense physical and emotional relationship. Two years later, when the American who had brought Charlie out of the closet went back to the States, Charlie was heartbroken. Afterward, his romantic preference remained fixed exclusively on Western men, a proclivity, he said, that was common among gay Thai men. About three years later, Charlie's wife found out he was gay, and she divorced him to marry another man, taking the children with her. Charlie attempted suicide by taking sleeping pills, but was found by a neighbor and his stomach was pumped. Upon recovering, he moved to Bangkok and lived in a cramped apartment shared by four other men. Now, he made a scant living as a caretaker of the garden of a wealthy Thai businessman.

"Now I meet you," Charlie said, concluding his story. His eyes looked dark black and pained. "This is the first time in two years I feel so good. I think I love you baby . . . stay here."

"Charlie, we just met," I began. "I'd like to stay here a long time, but—"

"No money," finished Charlie.

"Right...I'm out, you're out. We only have enough for two more nights together."

"Two nights not enough. I get money, you stay ten day, okay?"

"Okay." I smiled and squeezed Charlie's hand. We found a cheaper hotel and spent the night making sweetest love as crickets chirped softly outside.

\* \* \* \*

When I awoke after a couple hours of deep sleep, Charlie was gone. The desk clerk could only say Charlie would "come back soon." I began to mull over how the money I had had wired to Hong Kong might be routed to Bangkok so I could stay longer. Logistically, it was impossible in so short a time.

In the late afternoon I was forced by hunger to go out for something to eat. When I returned to the room, I found Charlie sitting on the bed with a strapping blond Australian in his late thirties. Unsure of why the Australian was there, I introduced myself and chatted a minute. Finally I just came out with it and asked, "Okay, what's going on here?"

The Australian jumped up. "I've got to go for a while," he said. "See you in a bit." He hastened out.

"I no want hurt you," Charlie said.

"Uh-huh," I said, with immediate dread. "But?"

Increasingly agitated, Charlie explained he had gone out after I fell asleep, borrowed more money and lost it in yet another card game. He had by chance met the Australian to whom, he said, "I sell the body, get money for you and me stay." He said the man had offered to support him and live with him for a month, an offer which, since Charlie was still broke and I had to leave, he was tempted to take. "I no want to hurt . . . I am not bad man . . . but . . . I fuck you over, I know. I feel bad."

My face filled with hot blood. I stared hard at him. "You are fucking me over!" I shouted, "How can you . . ." He slumped in his chair, so utterly dejected I couldn't go on.

"I no like. I am sorry." Charlie was near tears. "I am lonely. You stay only two nights or ten days, then go. I need somebody when you gone. I love you, not him. When I have sex with him, I tell him I love you."

"Oh come on! How can you drop me for this guy and still sit there and say you love me? You're just hustling—" I felt anger, but also like I was being mean.

"Ohhh . . . I go crazy!" Charlie grabbed his head with his hands and pulled it down to his knees. "I love you. No love him. I sleep him for money. Yes, he good-looking, but I no love for him. Want you. But you go . . ." A tear fell from his eye.

"But . . . if you stay with him, then I have no reason to stay . . . even if I could get money for a few days more."

"What I should do?" Charlie asked earnestly, his eyes now streaming tears.

"You're a man, do what you want," I said angrily, with regret of being mean in my anger.

Charlie took a deep breath and said, "I go with him."

There was a rap at the door and the Australian entered, sitting on the edge of the bed next to Charlie. I was slouched sullenly in my chair.

"Look, I'm sorry," the Australian said to me. "I really feel bad. I mean taking him away from you for what little time you have together."

"You're not taking him away. He's going because he wants to."

"I'm alone here!" Charlie said hotly. "You go away! Some other place. Some other boy. He stay. I need love Western man."

"Look, Charlie," said the Australian with considerable tenderness, "don't you see that as long as you love only foreigners this is going to happen?"

"Too late. Already I only love Western man."

"Yeah," said the Australian, "but you'll just go from one man to the next and the next and the next. You'll always be hurt at the end of a month or two."

Charlie leaned against the big blond man, stretching his own shorter legs out in order to put them across my knees, as if trying to bridge us all. I glared at him and said, "Charlie, for someone who claims to be in love with me, you sure enjoy sharing yourself with somebody else—*right in front of me.*" I stopped speaking. Seeing the pain on Charlie's face, I suddenly believed him, felt ashamed, and refrained from making any more hurtful remarks. "No point in it," I thought dejectedly.

Charlie looked sharply and deeply at me. "Please, *please,* you no hate me."

His gaze pierced my heart. I wondered if I was compassionate or just a sucker, but managed to say, "No Charlie, I don't hate you."

"You still write me from America?"

"Yeah, Charlie, I'll write you."

"Well, mate, let's go," said Charlie's new friend.

As they stood and went to the door, Charlie turned and said, "Good-bye Rick." His eyes were tearful, red, and bloodshot. I recalled with alarm that he had once tried suicide when his wife left him

"Good-bye Charlie . . . don't worry . . . it's okay." I felt a rent in the pit of my stomach as they walked out, leaving the door open.

As evening came on, alone in the room, my heart was heavy. My eyes burned. The euphoria of the last two days gave way to an equal despair. I packed mechanically, set the alarm, checked my new plane reservation, and went to bed. I sweated through anxious, troubled sleep, wondering what was the point of it all.

Just at dawn, before the alarm awoke me, there was a knock at the door.

"This Charlie."

I jumped up. "Come in." I opened the door guardedly.

Charlie stepped into the room. We threw our arms around each other. After an awkward moment, with pressed his face into my chest, he gasped, "I'm *sorry*."

"I'm sorry too, Charlie." I hugged him hard. I put my lips on his hair, rested my cheek on his head. Suddenly I felt Charlie's hot tears dripping down my chest and stomach. My own eyes filled with tears and a lump came to my throat. We sat holding each other, each knowing the other understood.

Finally it was time to go. Letting go of him, releasing his embrace as he released mine, was one of the saddest moments of my life. That physical and psychic separation said good-bye more poignantly than any words could. My last sight of him was waving at me from the step of that little hotel.

As I rode to the airport in the taxi I pulled out a snapshot Charlie had given me with his address on back. He was shirtless, in blue jeans, smiling broadly while sitting on the back rail of a ferryboat, white sand and turquoise beach behind him. I wondered what Western boyfriend might have taken this photo, and hoped the boundless happiness expressed by that smile would someday again return to Charlie, and perhaps again to me.

# ☙ 4    Running with the Bull:
## A Madrid Romance

*Gabriel Schael*

### Barbara De Angelis's Wish List

Traveling abroad is a good way to heal a broken heart. Another summer romance has ended, and my only consolation is a round-trip ticket to the homeland of San Fermin, Picasso, Salvador Dali, and flamenco. Not to mention the beautiful dark looks of the Spanish people. I'm hoping a drop into another culture will shake off the mental constraints of my daily routine, help clear my thoughts and feelings, and soothe the wounds suffered by another failed relationship. When you travel, you can't help but collide right into yourself—a self without the distractions of hometown baggage.

My mother, who has the energy of a hurricane, owns a gay and lesbian tour company and has convinced me (it didn't take long) to help her lead a tour to the gay capitals of Spain, a visit to the beautiful cities of Barcelona, Sitges, Seville, Madrid, and the Valley of Penedes, the wine region of the North. Does it really matter that I don't speak Spanish?

Eager to leave a small part of me behind, the part that hurts, I embark on the adventure with a small suitcase, a Buddhist prayer book, a bottle of vitamins, maps, itinerary, a Spanish dictionary, and a pink paperback copy of Barbara De Angelis's *The Real Rules: How to Find the Right Man for the Real You.* I rip off the pink cover from embarrassment. At this point, I'm accepting all the advice I can get, even if in secret. As a silly little exercise in the power of intention at the guru's

*Looking for Love in Faraway Places*
© 2007 The Haworth Press, Inc. All rights reserved.
doi:10.1300/5366_04

suggestion, I write a list of the attributes of my ideal partner—the one I haven't met yet. Be specific, Barbara advises. So I am. Right down to accent, intellect, heart, personal interest, values, style, height, hair color, and the way he looks when he smiles. Wishful thinking perhaps, but like Plato's theory of forms, if we can imagine it, it must therefore exist.

This much I know: He won't be an American.

### Duty Free Love and All that Hype

I retrace my roots in Madrid, eager to match the city with the countless tales my mother shared growing up. She has fond memories of her time spent in Madrid as a child. It was my grandfather's unfulfilled wish that all his daughters marry solid Spanish men. After leaving Madrid, they chose to ignore his advice, instead sprinkling across the American states, mingling in and finally settling with American men. Maybe I'll have better luck in Madrid, though it won't exactly be what my grandfather had in mind.

Madrid is magnificent. The wide boulevards and the regal architecture, a society clued into the rules and benefits of fashion that allude most Americans, street vendors selling roasted chestnuts and steaming corn, and flocks of agitated pigeons soaring over statues of muscular, chiseled male gods who stand guard atop the rooftops of ornately designed buildings. The terra-cotta-colored apartments, faded yellow, deep reds, and browns, tall and narrow, lean in toward me, defying gravity. It all takes my breath away. This city is vibrant and alive with every turn I make, everywhere I look. I people watch in the Plaza Mayor, drinking Sangria and sampling tapas, and allow my American sensibilities to slip away.

A few rules and tips for a tourist to abide by in Madrid: Be prepared to walk. The streets overflow with the brisk pace of all ages, no matter what the hour. Be prepared to eat dinner after 10:30 pm. Patience is required. Animated conversation rules supreme, so if you're dining with a Spaniard be prepared for the meal to stretch on for hours. This is not a fast-food nation (at least not yet). Be prepared to put a little effort into the way you dress. Makeup for a woman and dark socks for a man a must. Never wear white socks unless you want to give away your birthplace—especially white socks with sandals. (Not that I ever wore white socks with sandals.) Be prepared to fall in love with siesta. It's in place for a reason—catching a rest to make up for Spanish socializing that can last into the wee hours of the morning. The Spanish work to live not live to work. And be prepared to tolerate the lingering, invasive, permeating smell of cigarette smoke. You can't escape it. Not within the stuffiness of fine dining, tightly packed bars, or four-star-hotel elevators. Spain is a tobacco company's wet dream. Complaining about it won't help. I usually give in, waiting to ventilate my lungs when I return to the States. The warmth of the Spanish people overcompensates for the lack of a smoke-free zone. All in all, it's a quality of life I wish I had back home.

## At First Sight

I notice him in line.

The Madrid chill cuts to the bone as the group I am touring with waits in line for Liquid, a gay, neon-infused video bar located close to the Gran Via, the busy vein of this thriving capital. We huddle as best we can in our LA clothing—meaning we look good but we may as well be wearing sheer stockings for the effectiveness in keeping out the biting wind of October.

Tipping the six-foot scale, jet-black hair, gelled and slicked in a subtle postpunk style, dressed up in euro-trash denim that is all the Madrid rage, with full lips, ivory skin, and chiseled features, he passes the huddled and impatient and is ushered in by the doorman like Spanish royalty. He is what I would call the quintessential Spanish babe.

A half hour later I'm straining to aim my camera over the sandwiched crowd, realizing how much no matter what continent I am on, gay bars all look pretty much the same. I leap up and down. "What are you doing?" my friend Harley asks, trying to balance two lemon and vodka drinks. "It's not even a good song."

"I'm trying to take a picture of that guy." I point him out. "Why not just introduce yourself? It's easier and more fulfilling." After ten

minutes pass and I still haven't put a foot forward, my travel companions begin egging me on. "Go on! Go say hi. Go on! Go say hi!" It's
like a mantra chant. I shake my head vigorously. "No. No. No. Don't
push me." I just want to admire from afar. One step at a time, please.
The Spanish Stranger hasn't even looked my way. My group gives up
on me. It's time to move on to the next club, anyway. "Well, if it's
meant to be you'll see him again," a Stoic in the group adds. Not
likely, I think to myself. Chueca is a gay city-within-a-city with many
bars and clubs to choose from on a Saturday night.

### As Fate Would Have It…

We head to Polana, a thumping, cavelike dwelling where the natives party to 1950's American rock 'n' roll and Spanish dance hits.
Drag queens blow me kisses and I smile weakly as I try to find the
exit. The wave of separation from my ex-boyfriend has just crashed,
tearing my newly recovered self to wet, teary shreds. (I was not really
spilling tears, but with another round of cocktails I just might have.
That would have certainly unnerved the group. I was not about to
take any chances.)

"I'm going back to the hotel," I tell Harley. He threatens me with a
mock slap to the face.

"This is your last weekend in Madrid. Don't let your mind get the
best of you." Good advice. I'm still headed in the direction of the exit.
"What would you like right now more than anything?" he asks me,
right on my heel.

"Nothing. A warm bed and—"

I'm suddenly speechless. He's standing right in front of me, the one
that caught my eye, the Spanish Stranger. I take a deep breath, which
sounds more like a gasp. He smiles down at me. I've completely forgotten what's-my-ex, the memory of his face dissolving into tiny scattered fragments of nothingness.

"Are you leaving?" Is he speaking to me? I look behind me. Harley
has vanished. I have to get a grip. Fast.

"Are you talking to me?"

He laughs.

"You are American?" He has a rich deep voice.

"How did you know?" I glance down at my socks, making certain I wore the dark ones.

"You speak English. And..." he pinches his nostrils and speaks through the nasally voice "The way you speak." His eyes are gentle. He's not trying to be rude. "All Americans speak this way." He motions to the throat. "They speak from here. The Spanish speak from here." He motions to the gut.

His arm is around my waist. "Do you have a boyfriend?" he asks.

"No."

"Good."

It's decided. I stay. It's amazing how fast a mood can change.

His name is Manuel. It turns out his English matches my grasp of the Spanish language: severely limited. We batter and beat our rebellious sentences to obey. We depend on our eyes, smiles, and hand gestures for meaning. After a night of dancing he walks me to my hotel holding hands, something I wouldn't dare do in the States. People on the street don't seem to mind or even notice. We're just two young men taking a night stroll together. He leaves me at the lobby with an invitation to dinner.

I keep myself out of the hotel the next day touring the city. I want to avoid the disappointment of the silent phone zone. I want to leave Madrid with the memory of a brief sweet encounter. It's better that way. Leave on a high note.

After a long day of sightseeing and shopping I return to retrieve my key from the front desk. My thoughts are already on the packing I have to do for my early morning flight. The tidy female concierge has a message for me.

"Someone has been waiting for you." She taps her watch with a reproachful look.

Manuel leaps from lobby sofa. *"Hola!"* I'm completely taken back. He actually showed up. He taps his watch referring to the time. *"Malo, malo.* You are a bad boy." He flashes a smile that guarantees a late checkout.

We spend the next few hours lost in the city, searching for the perfect spot to enjoy my last night in Madrid. I'm usually reserved on first dates. However, something takes hold of me. I do something I've never done before. I take his hand and kiss his palm tenderly. He later tells me that was the moment he fell in love. He removes a bracelet from his wrist, a gift from his father on a visit to Cuba, and places it on my wrist. "So you don't forget me."

### Dodging Cupid's Arrow

He wants to know, demands to know, when I plan on returning to Spain. When can he see me again? I'm not sure, knowing it's not any time soon, but to relax him, to relax us both, I tell him in June. I don't really plan on returning in June, but it's something to say. He sighs. There are tears in his eyes. I'm amazed someone can feel so strongly and have no qualms about showing it. We're sitting on a park bench. He stares out in the distance, thinking something through, then comes to some conclusion. He takes my hand and says, "I will wait for you." He's serious. I smile. This is very sweet and so very unrealistic. I'm reminded of Toto proclaiming his love in the confessional booth to his unmoved object of desire in the film *Cinema Paradiso*. I'm going to savor this moment.

"I don't understand this," he continues, "but I think I love you." For someone who just came out of a disappointing relationship, who no longer wants to wear his heart on his sleeve, and who has decided to purchase the concrete for the wall that will encircle his heart, this confession of love was a bit much for me to take without an inner grin and condescending pat to the shoulder. Sure, you love me. After a few hours spent dancing, strolling, and barely understanding each other, suddenly you're in love with a foreigner that doesn't even speak your language. But I understand infatuation. We both obviously hit a spark with each other. Who was I to wipe the tears from his soulful, romantic eyes with a rough rag of reality? I keep my thoughts to myself.

In the cab, he watches me from the window, the tears still at a flow.

This is a nice way to end the trip. Maybe one day I will see him again. If not, at least I have a wonderful memory. At the airport my gift bracelet explodes off my wrist and twenty beads go scattering across the terminal elevator. "There goes your relationship." Harley says.

## Twenty-First Century Postal Overdrive

From the moment I get off the plane the international phone calls begin. Limited conversation to be sure, but he has the I-need-you-and-love-you delivery line perfected like a true Romeo. I've experienced the passionate natures of the Southern Europeans before, very different from the generally reserved, cool mode of my fellow Angelenos. Rarely has passion of this nature ever crossed the Atlantic as a carry-on in Delta before.

What follows is six months of beautifully written letters pledging eternal love, detailed in vibrant colors of ink; gifts in crinkled brown wrap parcels containing funny drawings, snapshots, and childhood photos of Manuel and his family; phone calls on the weekends; and e-mails during the week. His English begins to improve. "I'm learning for you." He tells me. We're moving on from the see-Jane-run style of communicating. He's very determined, and it is all so terribly romantic. I'm flattered and intrigued. Above all I'm puzzled. Why is he putting so much effort into pursuing someone he only met once, someone who lives out of the country, across that little body of water called the Atlantic, at the very far side of the United States? Are the pastures that dry in Madrid? Why am I so doubtful? Am I jaded? Don't I believe in that love-at-first-sight bit anymore? Perhaps he's faced the same difficulty I experienced from dating in my own backyard. I really have no idea. I decide to take it all with a grain of salt. This is a nice distraction, an abstract dating situation for the mind alone, but not really a part of my daily life.

## Love at 190 MPH

Surprisingly, after six months, my prediction comes true. I end up back in Madrid, just as I had promised but never really believed possible. I'm leading a group of restless Americans on a tour to Ibiza, ending in a climatic finale at Gay Pride Madrid. The buildup is exciting and nerve-wracking. These past months I've forged a written bond with Manuel. I wonder how that connection will hold up in person.

Our reunion takes place during the prime hour of Madrid's Gay Pride: chaos with spirit! A large percentage of the 500,000 gathered aren't all of the gay persuasion. The Spanish aren't one to turn down any excuse for a party. Gay pride is just one more celebration to add to the plethora of monthly festivals and religious holidays.

Climbing over parked cars because there is no room to walk, trying not to spill the big-gulp size sangria in the paper cup provided by the friendly outdoor drinking booths on every corner is a great way to get to know someone. We're like first-date lovers in the midst of an intoxicated revolution. He embraces me before I slip off the roof of the car, holds me tight, and tells me he's so happy his "boyfriend" is finally here.

This dramatic opening segues right into another as we set off on a quiet journey by train for the enchanted Hanging City, more commonly known as Cuenca. The time spent holding back dizziness on the world's slowest train is worth it as we arrive during the magic hour of dusk. We check into a converted monastery nestled high along the cliff's edge and continue the process of getting to know each other. It doesn't take long to realize that despite the cultural differences, we are similar in many ways.

Not daring to find out how conservative a former monastery can be by requesting a King, we fight to make our two twin beds into one big one by pushing the mattresses together and stretching the single sheet out (doesn't fit). We fall through the cracks several times, hitting our backs against tile floor, and finally have to rearrange the beds horizontally. After a long weekend, as we lay side by side, our feet dangling off the ends of the bed, hands locked together, Manuel looks me straight in the eye and demands the following if we are to continue:

1. I must promise to be faithful to him. Distance and length of time spent apart is no excuse for infidelity.
2. I must promise to make every effort to see him. Our holidays are to be spent together.

3. I must promise to fight for our relationship against any future obstacles (whatever that means).
4. I must promise to move to Spain.

"I've make this promise to you, Gabriel. And?"

And he sure doesn't waste anytime. He waits for my response. Well, this is certainly different from what I'm used to dealing with when dating in LA. Usually, it's "Let me see how I can fit you around my schedule. My life is my life, your life is yours. Any objections? Yes? Don't be needy and please don't project."

I'm hesitating. I fidget with my wallet, pulling out Barbara De Angelis's list, folded like a tight, forgotten origami. I read it over. I look up. Look down. Look up. It's him. I've received exactly what I had asked for . . . right down to the last period. He's finally materialized. He fits the picture and shares my values, carefree spirit, and passion. Here is someone who lives by the ideals I used to believe in but compromised long ago and readjusted and discarded to fit the survival dating scene. With his guidance, those ideals can be rediscovered, dusted off, polished, and given permission to take flight. He promises to meet me with an equal amount of fire from the heart.

I take a deep breath then take my oath.

## *Jet-Setter Blues*

Over the next two years we meet each other across the world, whenever we can, however we can. Not that that we have the funds to play Paris Hilton, only the intense desire to make each visit happen somehow puts things into motion, decimating logic and both our bank accounts. By sacrificing the usual toys and gadgets, like the new car I desperately want, along with the benefits of working for a tour company, I always seem to be able to manage a visit. We don't always have luxury of a private room instead having to opt for the budget crunch of sharing a room with family or friends, or the simple ambience of a pension, but we adapt and make it work. Little by little we meet each other's worlds.

Farewells are always sad, tear filled, and long. I miss my flight almost every single time visiting him, like some Freudian slip of the ticket. This way we are granted one more day to spend with each other, which turns out to usually be our most intimate, quiet, and memorable time spent together. Yet, it always ends much too soon, just when we are beginning to settle into a perfect groove of synchronicity, leaving behind the initial awkwardness of being reunited after so long.

The touchdowns back home are the worst for me. I imagine the LAX landing strip littered with used Botox needles, celebrity headshots, and shattered apple martini glasses and steroid vials. I see only the worst my city has to offer. I see a life without Manuel.

The months apart are a flux between good moments (friends help) and extreme loneliness (which friends can't help). I'm in boyfriend mode, yet can't reach out and touch him. My senses are alive and I have only the telephone and black cyberspace of e-mail to sustain it. There are moments when I ask myself, "What am I doing? Why am I in a monogamous relationship (which equals celibacy) with a man I can't see? What is the point?" I fight off small frantic bouts of anxiety and depression. Somehow, those emotional spells ease out and calm with a phone call, his comforting words. Then once again I am at the terminal, reuniting with him. And my doubts are extinguished in one swift embrace.

### Just What Are You?

People have a hard time classifying me. I'm not single...yet my boyfriend isn't around. I'm like a strange half-breed. People's reactions always interest me when I tell them I'm in a monogamous long-distance relationship. Some think it's romantic. Some think it's ridiculous. Some are quick to point out it's a waste of time and a waste of the attractive years. I've even come across some hostile reactions with the "One of you is obviously cheating. There's no way you're being faithful." Some tell me I'm avoiding having to deal with a real relationship.

Bottom line is, I think it says more about them than it does about me.

## Crossroads

We lay in a slumped sofa bed listening to the grunts and moans of heavy lovemaking. It plays out in stereo through the flimsy stucco walls. We're in Ibiza sharing a two-bedroom home with six of Manuel's friends. Anna is the mother of Manuel's best friend. She likes smoking pot and having sex with her tan, fur-coated Greek boyfriend with the bedroom door open. Her squeals are loud and animal like. I try to focus on the question at hand.

"Do you love me?" Manuel asks. The headboard thumps against the wall. Or maybe it's her head.

"Of course I do."

A grunt. A squeal. The wall shudders.

"Where do we go from here? We need our life together, Gabriel. We need our privacy. How much longer can we do this?"

I know he's referring to more than having our own hotel room.

## The Announcement

It's Christmas Eve at Manuel's home. Like many Spanish men in their twenties, he still lives at home with his family. They don't know he's gay. I find this hard to believe considering he practically has a shrine dedicated to me in his bedroom, a wall plastered with only pictures of me. He remains adamant the family has no idea. Who can his mother possibly think I am?

Looking like a Coppola Godfather epic, Manuel's family gathers together for a three-day feast in a small dining room: parents, grandparents, aunts, uncles, cousins, in-laws. And this is only one side of the family. They are full of hugs and laughter. Not a word of English spoken. I just nod my head and return the smiles. I genuinely like his family.

His mother acts like some mad Julia Child whipping up dish after dish in a frenzy to feed all the children of Europe. She dotes on me, insisting I try every dish, ruffling my hair, waiting for my expression of taste bud ecstasy. When she's not looking I steal kisses with her son.

As I'm in the process of stuffing myself with a dish I thought was the main meal but is in fact only the appetizer, his family becomes absolutely silent. Manuel has just spoken. All eyes are on the both of us, puzzled if not a bit worried. "What did you tell them, Manuel?" He wears a mischievous grin.

"That I am moving to Los Angeles to live with you."

A dish drops in the kitchen.

### When Worlds Collide

Moving in with me to play house is not the explanation he gives his family. Rather, he's going for the opportunity to work with my mother's tour company, who has quickly adopted him as her poster child. His overprotective mother, fearful of losing her son to foreign, unknown soil, consults her psychic to see if this is a good idea. She's told with all assurance of white magic that it is.

I doubt the psychic told her he would be sharing my bed.

It's an easy transition for Manuel. He adapts to life in my city with its rules of a convalescent home. It may as well be considering the nights begin and end early. Everything closed by two a.m. Dinner by eight p.m. No more siestas, no more six a.m. barhopping. Worse still, he is aghast at the cut to his freedom to smoke. It's an unheard of concept to have laws to prevent smoking. It's a daily struggle for Manuel to accept that there will be no more lighting up in restaurants and bars, chilling with a drink and a smoke. He pleads to allow him to smoke in the bedroom. Grudgingly I allow this. I can't strip him of all his comforts.

A city center is missing. Los Angeles is a string of suburbs connected by sidewalks and streets devoid of plazas and people walking. He finds the interaction between people in L.A interesting. Why do we greet each other with such enthusiasm "Hello! How are you?!" when we really aren't looking for a detailed answer? There's no follow-up permitted. He learned this the hard way when people's eyes glazed over and they seemed uncertain how to handle his lengthy, honest reply. From friends to the local grocer, in Spain it's common to greet each other with fifteen minutes worth of catch-up in each other's lives, while we tend to be friendly on the surface and preoccupied with our time beneath. Still, he admits it's easier to meet people in the States. The Spanish are reserved about inviting someone to their home, but once the invitation is in place you know you have a friend for life.

He also finds it amusing that we place a great importance on the cars we drive, shiny and expensive, but live in a small rental apartment. We hold a great stake in appearances. Generally, we are health obsessed, prizing our gym memberships, and conscious of our status. Why care more for what you drive than where you live, he asks? In Spain the goal is to put the investment in where you live not in what you drive.

He scolds me for throwing things away. He saves leftovers, everything from the last piece of bread in the wrapper to the oil used for cooking. When something is torn or broken, I tend to toss it. He retrieves it and mends it with needle and thread or finds another use for it. "It's so easy to get rid of things in the U.S. because you can easily go out and replace it. You don't take care of things to last. You consume, consume, and consume." His family and most people take care of purchased items as though it's the last one they will ever buy.

I notice my life is organized now. My wardrobe has expanded. Shirts are hung in the order of the correct color scheme. My night shorts and tank top is folded under my pillow for me to find at night. The kitchen has the aroma of Spanish-style cooking; extra virgin olive is a hot commodity in our place. My diet of chicken and brown rice seems pale to his cooking. The treadmill is my new best friend. While he takes smoking breaks in between our workouts, I push harder on the treadmill to offset the carb extreme, rich dishes and wines he serves in abundance. Waking up and finding him nestled in my arms each morning seems like nothing short of a miracle to me.

I can't imagine my life without him.

### *Uncle Sam's Twelve-Week Reality Check*

The country may be safer from terrorists (supposedly) but the realities of temporary visas, work permits, and lengthy stays in U.S. hit us like ice water. Immigration laws after 9/11 have become stricter. Manuel can visit the United States for ninety days. He can eventually return after another short visit. It's the back-and-forth syndrome, and with every return he is welcomed with an intensive interrogation at customs. Manuel is reluctant to admit to the men in uniforms that he is visiting his boyfriend and not in the business of blowing things up. We have been living together for over six months and our next deadline is fast approaching. Work is impossible for him to find without a working visa. Our options are limited. There are two ways he can remain longer than three months. A company can sponsor him for six months, which is not as easy as it sounds, or he can get married—to a woman. Since this is out of the question and gay marriage is still the one accepted and legal act of discrimination allowed and applauded by the majority, our options are rather limited. We're living together on borrowed time.

"What happens to us when they don't let me return?" he asks me. "We will both die. Our relationship will be over." He's always a bit dramatic, but he's not too far off. A long separation would definitely put a strain on our relationship. I worry a gay backlash might be gathering like a storm after the most recent presidential election. Any hope of domestic partnership is out the question, otherwise there would always be that option. Then Manuel takes me completely by surprise. He proposes to me. It's not a traditional, get-down-on-his-knee kind of a proposal, with a shiny ring in hand, soft candlelight in the background. No, it's more practical.

"If I can't return, then you have to come with me to Spain so I can marry you. Then you can live and work in Spain. We will be together." Spain recently has legalized gay marriage. It's a major step forward for Spain. Ironically, a country under the deep influence of the Catholic Church, that has only recently rid itself of the fascist grip of Franco, has made this progressive leap. America, the 200-year-old nation of democracy and freedom, where all men are created "equal," continues to uphold the "sanctity" of marriage, pushing with religious zeal and moral outrage antigay measures, stripping bare domestic partnerships, and attempting to amend the constitution to prevent any future possibility of a union between two people that don't fit the symbolic replica of Adam and Eve from marrying. Still, the morally righteous seem to have no problem with a spur-of-the-moment Las Vegas marriage blessed in an Elvis chapel. In America, married couples don't even have to live in the same house. Now that I am affected, I understand the fight for gay marriage, a civil rights issue that never concerned me before until now.

I accept Manuel's proposal. Come this summer, we will attend his sister's wedding in Spain. Unbeknownst to his family, and with the blessing of my mine, we will be celebrating two marriages. As his sister takes her oath to cherish and love her man unto death do they part, Manuel and I will be standing side by side, knowing that our own small private ceremony, with only our friends and my immediate family in attendance, holds just as much meaning and importance.

# Journey to the End of the Land

*Morris Kafka*

I have a snapshot dated August 19th, 1987. I'm twenty-one, standing in the street in New Brunswick, New Jersey, about to leave for Provincetown, at the edge of Cape Cod. I'm seeking a brief summer respite from the urban grit of the small college town I've been living in.

In 1983 I lived at home in quiet, suburban Maplewood, in one of countless quaint imitation colonials. At the time, I commuted via a well-worn public bus that crawled down Springfield Ave to Newark's New Jersey Institute of Technology, where I studied architecture. Ghetto blasters rocked us with dance and rap music as incense smoke wafted in from the sidewalks. Pushers wielded drugs while I hid behind books and stared at the bus's starburst-patterned ceiling, stifling from the diesel fumes. My secret joy was covertly observing the outfits and hairstyles of the passengers and listening to the happy music. When I got off the bizarrely festive bus I quickly walked the three decrepit blocks on Martin Luther King Boulevard trying not to look scared. Classes were in a dismal converted factory, and I was bothered by the irony of paying tuition to hear lectures about beauty and form in architecture in such a setting.

I soon realized we NJIT students were likely to end up starting at the low end of the totem pole in a large architectural firm rather than to use our creative abilities to design exciting buildings. The idea of doing mundane work for others to afford a staid life behind one of those Maplewood lawns was as stifling as the air in the bus. The professors and students were on another wavelength, and most ridiculed my interest in rehabilitating the interesting old buildings surround-

*Looking for Love in Faraway Places*
© 2007 The Haworth Press, Inc. All rights reserved.
doi:10.1300/5366_05

ing us. I knew I had to leave my studies in drab Newark. In January 1984 I moved on to the promise of studying art history at Rutgers University. I wasn't quite sure what career path this would lead to, but I followed my intuition.

Rutgers in the 1980s seemed filled with optimism, vitality, and energy. Student activism and diversity were celebrated and an environment of exploration was fostered. My parents helped me buy and renovate a Victorian home in a marginal neighborhood. I shared my house with a constantly changing cast of local characters. Befriending Jay, a tall, intense musician from my genealogy class, I was soon introduced to a nearby house full of artistic people. Terrie was studying painting and dance and she mesmerized me. We soon became very close. We'd dress all in black, our hair slicked back, and go dancing at parties and nightclubs where all kinds of people were welcomed, accepted, and appreciated into the celebratory atmosphere. Unconventionally beautiful, Terrie reminded me of the androgynous Annie Lenox.

Terrie often took me to a little brick-walled nightclub in an old converted storefront. Upbeat music played nonstop and the small dance floor was often filled. It was mostly gay and friendly, and we were comfortable there. Out back was a little walled garden where I kissed a man for the first time. One night, someone danced up to me and soon I had a new friend, named Ali. With big green eyes, smooth skin, and dark hair, he was full of energy laughing, cheering and dancing all the time as he wove his way into my life. When finances became tight for him, he left his high-rise apartment and rented a room in my house. Before I really knew what hit me, he had become my new lover. While I was absorbing all of this, I went to Hawaii for vacation with my family and came home to find red hairs on my bed sheets. Housemates were soon complaining of pubic lice, and while cleaning up, I saw Ali had a bottle of lice shampoo. He denied being the source of the problem, but I was furious and told him to move out. He went on his knees to my best friend Brendan to beg him to intervene, but it was only years later that Brendan let me know of this.

I then had an affair with an intelligent, independent-thinking woman who was studying journalism. Rachel was energetic and we had fun going out dancing at fraternity parties, painting our apartments together, and going to Hillel and ethnic events. After a while, though, I noticed every conversation was mostly about her and she didn't seem too interested in me. I felt unappreciated and unwanted as she became fixated on Jake, a pleasant Israeli trucker with a scraggly beard. We spent less and less time with each other, and the affair ended rather quietly as she moved in with Jake.

My best friend Rita, who lived in an old house across the street, saw I was having a hard time romantically and decided a getaway to Provincetown was the cure. Though she had been there often, for me, Provincetown was a place for newlyweds. The black-and-white images in my parents' photo album showed a place from an old song, with clam chowder, sidewalk art, and shops where my mother bought ashtrays shaped like whales and seahorses. But what had always struck me were the images of the antique houses and the history the place was purported to hold. I agreed to go with her.

I packed my bag with preppy clothes and penny loafers. We set off in Rita's brown VW Rabbit with a few dollars and some disco cassettes for the six-hour drive to what seemed like the end of the planet. Our host was a vibrant woman living across from the bay in an old apartment. By the end of the trip it seemed Rita had introduced me to almost every lesbian in town. I spent some time alone at the beach and in the woods gathering my thoughts and went out dancing in the crowded clubs, but I felt like I was drifting along invisibly, observing this town from a hidden vantage point, unseen. Almost no one except Rita's friends talked to me. By the end of the week I packed up my inappropriate clothes and I was ready to go home. I had no idea that this was anything more than a novel excursion at the time.

Rita was dealing with her own relationship issues, and she left New Brunswick to rent a place in Provincetown that winter. I missed her dynamic company and set out on a long bus and train trip to see her for a week. The town was quiet and the tourists were gone, many of the shops were locked up. I met mostly locals and began to feel familiar with the place. Unlike the summer crowd, the men stared and flirted openly, even relentlessly— something I was not used to. I liked the attention and the off-season attitude and began to enjoy the place.

After graduating college in 1987, my previous social circle had dispersed and the clubs I had gone to were closing down. I had had little affection or sexual attention for a while.

Rita had her own ideas and took me house hunting. At that time the AIDS epidemic was devastating resorts with a high population of gay men. Many people were visibly ill and residents were leaving Provincetown in droves, saying the party was over. Still, Rita wanted to buy a house with me there. I was open to the idea, but we couldn't find something we could afford with our limited budgets. I went back to New Jersey and submerged myself in my work on old houses and community activism.

Soon after, Katie Anne, one of the women I had met in Provincetown, invited me back to stay at her antique home. I had my own truck and I loaded up tools and supplies and went regularly to visit her and do repair work on her house. A lovely host, she invited my dog Harvest to stay as well and encouraged me to date locally. Similar to the way that Rutgers drew me in as a student, I found this old town accepting me and celebrating my interests and differences. One day she offered to inexpensively rent me a large apartment in her home. My mother encouraged this as a good anecdote to the stress of my work in New Jersey. By October of 1992 I settled into a monthly commute between the two places.

I spent time fixing up my apartment and adjusting to Cape Cod life. I found some cafes and clubs and got to know the locals. A cheerful bartender at the ancient Atlantic House was especially friendly and encouraged me to come out more. One night as I was standing by a big timber pillar listening to the music, a guy walked up and leaned on the counter near me. He was wearing an old biker jacket with a button for a Colorado political initiative I had read about. Brent was from Cheyenne, Wyoming, and had arrived here from Denver and was now working as a waiter at the Townhouse. He was dark, scruffy, intense, and a bit scary looking but soft-spoken, polite, seemingly innocent, and close in age to me.

Though I never would have predicted it, there was immediately some heavy chemistry at work. Soon we were spending our free time together playing in the snow, biking, and walking my dog on the

beach. He expressed his love for me. Soon he moved into my apartment on a temporary basis. He was in a pinch. Like many working
people in Provincetown at this time he found that his inexpensive
rental was being sold to an upscale renovator. He did his best to be a
good housemate. He treated me to breakfast in bed, helped out
around the place, and took care of my dog when I was out of town.
Then one day I went out to lunch with a group of guys, some of whom
I had only recently met. Brent walked by the window in tight Levi's
501s without seeing me inside. One of the guys saw him and said,
"Check out the great ass on that guy." Someone else at the table responded, "I slept with him the other night," and the graphic detail
made it painfully obvious that he had. I sat silently, numbed, yet
feeling a familiar sinking feeling.

When confronted at home Brent was in complete denial but
turned red when I quoted the details. Deep down I thought this kind
of thing had been happening for a while. I recalled a night when a
beautiful full moon was visible from my bedroom windows, and Brent
said he was going out for cigarettes. I had waited up for a long while
and hardly slept, curled up, just feeling sad with my dog by my side.
Brent didn't return that night at all. The next day he told me he had
been hanging out and had accidentally fallen asleep at a friend's
house. Now it was all clear to me. I asked him to move out, but he
begged for a few days to find a place. Rentals were getting harder and
harder to find in town. Wealthier people were moving in as the town
came back into fashion, driving prices up. I made him give back the
key but allowed him to come in to sleep on the sofa temporarily. I
spent many late nights in anguish, on the phone for what seemed like
hours long distance to friends in New Jersey seeking solace and advice. Brent tried to patch it up, but it was too late. I felt hurt, unappreciated, and scared by his behavior.

In a selfish and mean-spirited move to give him a taste of his own
medicine I returned flirtations with a handsome, clean-cut young
man with wire-framed glasses. He was summering as a waiter at a local seafood house. I thought it was an omen that his name was also
Brent, though in appearance and demeanor he could not have been
more different. I told this new fellow what was going on in my life.

After going out dancing I took him home late one night, reiterating the context. My now ex-lover was waiting on the steps for me to open the door. He went to my stiff old sofa like a dog defeated after a fight while my guest and I went into the bedroom and closed the door. I felt horribly conflicted but I knew somehow I had to nail the lid shut on the old affair. This seemed to be the only way to get through to him.

The next morning, both Brents were gone from my place.

At this point, I felt pretty disgusted with my varied romantic attempts with both women and men. I was blessed with some very close friends, a busy career in home renovation and rentals, and a number of charitable and community causes. I immersed myself in these. I was never really lonely or bored. Life seemed fine except when I stopped to think how incomplete my soul felt. My dog was getting older but he still loved to take the trip back to Provincetown each month, he'd lie on the bench seat of the truck, his chin on my leg. At night, we'd walk along the bay. Watching the tide lap the shore and hearing the foghorns and the rigging slapping against the vessels in the bay was soothing. Harvest ran and played as I walked in the sand alongside. Yet even with the feeling of belonging in Provincetown, I still felt now as inexplicably isolated as I had in the staid suburbs of my youth.

Whoever decided who was on the A-list for social activities, it was not me. I knew many people and went to many functions but it seemed most everyone else had a mate or was being pursued by someone charming. I was left alone and attempts at conversation with people I found interesting were often rebuffed by their lack of interest. Not that there was a lack of people who flirted or were curious about me sexually. The town was small and people talked. People I hardly knew were familiar with intimate details of my life and sexual interests, but being a playboy was not my ultimate desire. I resented people who courted me in the guise of romantic interests when they saw me simply as a sex object, yet I realized I was guilty of the same behavior. It felt good to be asked to dinner, to be admired, to be seen publicly with people that were in my eyes attractive, and to have people trying to seduce me.

As AIDS continued to move through my world, my old friend Brendan became ill and asked to stay in Provincetown with me. He had worked for a major health and beauty company but moonlighted as a club disc jockey. He was popular, good-looking in a pale, vampirelike way, and somehow he always had an enthusiastic date. He encouraged me to talk to people, to ask both women and men out on dates, to keep my standards high, and to live life. I learned a lot about how to express myself from him. He was a bit worldlier than I was and a lot less uptight. Unfortunately, he'd exposed himself to all sorts of things that would be lethal later. He didn't get better while staying with me; he got worse. He withered enough that his father took him back to a hospital in New Jersey. Rita and I heard the phone ringing as we were in my driveway packing the car to go visit him on the day after Thanksgiving 1994. It was his folks. Brendan had just passed away. We gathered to spread his ashes at Herring Cove in Provincetown on a windy day, and I had been designated to organize the service. Reluctant to touch the ashes, I waded into the cold water to tip the urn. Brendan himself gave a final farewell gesture as the ashes were carried by a sudden turn of the wind, hitting me in my face, some going into my mouth. I had to laugh through my tears. His loss left another void in my life. I half waited for his usual antics, for him to call and ask me to go out for dinner at our favorite Italian restaurant with Rita. This loss was not first I knew from the epidemic, but it hit the closest.

It wasn't long after this that my dog Harvest, my sole remaining source of daily affection, now a nearly unheard of 18 years old, was gone. My previous lover Brent had been very close to Harvest. All three of us had shared my old brass bed on cold winter nights. By now, Brent had retreated to Denver from Provincetown. Shortly after we met, he had told some disturbing sexual stories of life as a young man in Wyoming, and I suggested he have an HIV test. The test came back positive. He was healthy, yet he refused to moderate his poor diet, smoking, or drinking. All these habits had created tension while we were dating and in later attempts at friendship, and I feared now they would weaken him further. He called often from Denver, sending snapshots of sunsets and greeting cards saying he was fine and still loved me and wanted to work things out. He had at least two lovers I knew of after our affair ended. One was with a man I knew in Provincetown who seemed to think he had caught a trophy in Brent and paraded it in my face when I happened to be somewhere they were. Later he asked quite seriously why I hadn't warned him of the heartache ahead from Brent.

Then one day Brent's mother called and told me the news. He had been much worse off than he said and had died in the hospital in Denver. When she visited his apartment, it had old photos of me all around. My name was the only one in his new little black book. As a memento she sent me some of his tight jeans and other clothes. Later she sent his ashes to be scattered in Provincetown. Some were scattered at Beech Forest, one of his favorite places, while some were saved for a waterside service at Herring Cove. His mother had longed for a proper Catholic burial for her firstborn but honored his requests. She cried on the phone to me that she had no grave to visit. As I went down to the pond in Beech Forest with another friend to scatter ashes I wondered how many other people's ashes have come home to Provincetown.

My friend Jason, a professional dancer with a young son, showed up at my gate about this time. He lived to dress up and go out on the town and we had paraded through the streets of Provincetown in all sorts of events wearing crazy costumes and dancing the nights away with the tourists. Jason encouraged me to meet new people and to keep open to a better love in my life. I knew he had been sick a while on that crisp day when he appeared. He placed a document on the shiny black leatherette cover of the bed of my truck and asked me to sign it. The white paper was in the direct glare of the bright Cape Cod sun but there I saw he had planned his own funeral. He had come to ask me to agree to be a pallbearer. It was most overwhelming, but I bit my tongue and signed. He must have known. Within months I found myself wearing white gloves at a Catholic mass for him and trying to lift my end of the casket without breaking down.

I could understand why so many people were still down on Provincetown as I saw it starting to come back into popularity. It seemed to be the vortex of doom even as the natural beauty and freedom beckoned me. Into all this sadness, my landlady informed me that she would need the apartment back so her lover could move in. I was unhappy, but thought maybe it was a sign to leave town. She had given me generous time to find another place if I chose to stay in the area. Going back to New Jersey in my truck felt like leaving a friend behind. After a couple of weeks in New Brunswick I wanted to walk on the bay again and smell the salt air. Provincetown had been completely under my skin for a long time, even as I tried to deny it. So I returned for a visit, staying on my old sofa, which was now in use at my friend Gillian's house. My friend Tony offered me a room in his place on the West End for the summer. It was cheap and it was adequate. My friend Jose needed a place so we shared the room. The situation resulted in a number of comical episodes that centered on figuring out how one of us could entertain a date while having some privacy. Eventually I found a cute apartment just around the corner from the local gathering spot, Spiritus Pizza. It had views of the bay and was in a classic Cape Cod house. It was a two bedroom, and Jose agreed to share it with me.

Things seemed to be falling into place as I spent time sorting through possessions and refinishing old furniture for the apartment. My parents came up to town and we had a house warming and birthday party in September of 1996. The winter passed relatively quietly but spring brought me two "marriage" proposals, both in the same week and both from far-flung men. Matt lived in LA and the other, Max, in Georgia. Both were kind, attractive, and romantic, yet I knew neither well. I was overwhelmed, feeling I had gone from the proverbial famine to the feast. Such far-flung affairs were impractical and I harbored no great hope, but I had feelings for them and kept in touch with both for a long time.

Locally though, the more I tried to be open to dating and the more I articulated the desire for a serious companion, the fewer people I met. It seemed that being clear about what I wanted eliminated people quickly. Somehow I became more sexually desirable, too. I got hit on more often than ever, but rarely got asked to dinner. When I asked people out on a date, they gave lame excuses or acted highly inappropriately. I watched dates openly flirting with other people, treating me poorly, or simply not reciprocating with an invitation to go out again. It seemed an exercise in futility. I had an illumination and realized it was time to just enjoy everything wonderful about my life. It was time to just keep meeting people without worrying about romance, to keep believing that it would happen if and when it was meant to.

A friend told me that I would not be able to take a lover until I decided to live in just one place. He asserted that no one could go out with someone who monthly commuted between homes in New Jersey and Massachusetts. It was this cut-and-dried point of view that brought me to my epiphany. I was not coming to Provincetown simply to escape work or to find a lover; the town of Provincetown was my affair in itself. Walking along the bay listening to the water lap the sand, hearing the now comforting dialects of the locals, smelling the beach roses in the heat of the summer, walking barefoot to the ocean through the tidal pools, sitting on a terrace with a cold drink looking at the beautiful sunset over the water, these were the things that made life worth living. Alone or with a companion, these priceless things I had every day I was in Provincetown.

I had made my peace with the town and no longer needed to impress anyone or strive to fit in or find the right parties. It just didn't matter anymore. I was simply happy to be alive and to celebrate being there. Into this newly renovated mental space like a miracle came a new set of people who shared love and support even as old friends left town. On a cold winter night my neighbor Joe would make a dinner, put logs on the fire, and invite me over. I'd bake a pie and have him over on another night. My new housemate Charles, a chef, and his lover Rob would offer delightful food and ask for my company out to eat. The folks at the Universalist Meeting House never went a week without some kind of social event into which I was always welcomed. Back in New Jersey, the old nightclubs did little for me, but my core group of friends continued to gather for celebrations. Life was quiet and nurturing.

At the beginning of 2004 I felt a shift that was hard to explain in concrete terms. Something inside me said this was a year for growth and change. I was afraid to acknowledge that I sensed a mate was going to arrive soon, but I felt it strongly and expressed it to a couple of close friends, even as I was afraid to fall into a trap with this thought. I had experienced a couple of pleasant, functional affairs over the past years, but nothing that grew into full or lasting romance. Then it happened. I went to meet friends out one spring night and I saw him. I just saw him and felt something. He didn't seem to notice me but I didn't need to pursue him.

Later that evening I was at Spiritus Pizza with the hungry crowds exiting the nightclubs of Provincetown. Only one seat was open on the bench out front. I asked the woman if it was taken and she told me to sit down. Then suddenly I felt something twitch inside me. I turned around and there he was again. It happened to be the case that everyone else on that bench was one of his friends. I started to get up to give him the seat when I saw him carrying food toward them, motioning to offer him the seat. He said I should stay seated. After a moment of silence, I looked at him again and a little voice in my head told me not to be shy—nothing ventured, nothing gained. I motioned to my lap and told him to come over and sit down, and to our mutual amazement he did.

Randy was an artist at heart, wonderfully able to express himself in his writing and a man of clarity and dignity. Both of us were content as people. Neither of us was consciously looking for a lover, yet we found something in one another that is very powerful. This feeling informs my daily existence as it contributes to my life. For the first time in a long time I felt a complete and abiding love that came from him and from me. My journey to the end of the land had brought me home.

# Marcelo

*Michael Mele*

Marcelo had tiny feet. I noticed as he was calling a cab for me. His toes were short. The nails were shallow. The feet themselves were pretty, but petite.

His dick wasn't. It wasn't gargantuan, but it was more than respectable. (So much for the unscientific correlation between foot size and cock size.) And it was very hard, standing unsupported at a one o'clock angle even before we got into bed (pretty respectable for our over-forty age cohort). Mine too was raring to go: the thin skin at the top of the shaft tingled like it was about to rip.

I'll always remember how sensitive Marcelo was. Wherever I touched him he squirmed. That drove me to touch him more and everywhere. *What about here? And what about there?* I thought as I drew designs on his torso, his knees, his back, and his neck with my finger. I didn't say it out loud, however, because he didn't speak English.

\* \* \* \*

We were three American tourists at the Titanic Club on Avenida Callao. We had been there before dinner, at eight o'clock, still not adjusted to the late socializing schedule in Buenos Aires. We had sat alone drinking cocktails while the barmen mopped the floor and Windexed the mirrors. So we went to the Palermo district for a steak dinner, then returned at eleven thirty, assuming that the place would be packed by then. Maybe seven guys lined the bar. There were plenty of empty stools for us despite a sandwich board at the door promising "dancers" at midnight. Still feeling out of synch with the local timetable but unsure of where else to go for some lively activity, we decided to stay. We had only a week in Argentina; no sense heading back to our hotel rooms so early. The bartender, who recognized us from before, greeted us with a big, white, blacklight smile. Perhaps we made a little scene, three chicas new to town, flipping through the menu for a cocktail, trying to translate from the Spanish, flirting with the barman. We were probably a frivolous spectacle, encouraged by feeling all the eyes of the small crowd on us, the newcomers.

After asking Ricky the barman to make me his own special cocktail I glanced to my left where a small man with curly black hair sat smiling in amusement. I caught his eye and joined his smile, then turned back to my friends. But curiosity pulled me immediately back to my left where the man was sipping from his glass. I laughed and he blinked at me. Boldly, I shifted my stool closer to him.

"*Buenas noches,*" I said. Back home in New York I would never have made a bold move like that, at least not so soon after making eye contact. But being away from everything familiar made me less inhibited. "*Cómo está?*"

Now I had exhausted my Spanish vocabulary. Demurely he answered with what I assumed meant "Pretty good, how about you?" Hmmmm. Now what? Ricky saved me by delivering my special cocktail of the house, an iridescent cream in a glass shaped like a flower vase. "A Golden Cadillac" he beamed. Oh well, so much for an exotic South American cocktail. I accepted the vase, sipped it, and quickly gave the approval he was waiting for. My two friends, who had ordered Quilmes beers, showered me with love in the form of ridicule. So I turned away from them, back to the man on my left who nodded amusement. I held out my Cadillac to toast his glass.

"*Agua,*" he shrugged, exhibiting his glass, but he toasted me all the same. We drank. I offered him a taste of my cocktail for which he had to drag his stool closer to mine.

By now I could hear my friends behind me digging into a discussion of their lives and relationships back home. I'd heard it all before, so I continued amusing myself by trying to converse some more with my new friend. Ah, where to begin?

"*Hablas inglés?*" I asked.

"No."

*"Italiano?"*

"No. *Francés?"* he offered. Well, if I could remember enough of my college French that might work.

*"Comment t'appel, tu?"* I asked.

"Um, Marcelo." Then he pointed to me—I guess that was the extent of his French.

"Michael," I said.

*"Bueno, bien!"*

And then, I don't know how it happened, we just plunged into a conversation in pidgin Italian, Spanish, French, and plenty of gesticulation. I learned where he was from, what he did, told him about our sightseeing plans for the week, and then suddenly we kissed. It came from nowhere. Unpremeditated. I was so exuberant over being able to understand him that it just happened. He was delighted and giggled, his black curls bouncing. We talked more, with fingers lightly resting on each other's knees. His smile was a waxing crescent throughout our banter. He polished off his agua and helped me with my Cadillac. Every time we made ourselves understood there was pure joy at the sense of accomplishment. I even noticed other guys around us getting caught up in our glee, smiling along with us.

"Michael," Steve tapped me on the shoulder. "We're leaving. Dennis is going home with a hustler and I'm going to an all night porn cinema."

I turned abruptly, sure he was kidding. "Oh, I think I'll stay," I said. "I want to wait for the dancers" (who were already a half hour late. I would never figure out this Argentine timetable). And there was Dennis kissing an extremely hunky man with arms the size of my thighs.

"Who's that?" I pointed at the man with my chin.

"That's the hooker Dennis met. They're going to a hotel around the corner. It's all right, I have his cell phone number and I negotiated the price for them."

Steve went to the men's room and Dennis drifted toward me with a florescent keyboard grin.

"Can you loan me fifty pesos?" he whispered. The hunk was talking with Ricky. I surreptitiously opened my billfold and handed him a banknote. In a moment they were gone and I turned back to Marcelo.

He was still there, looking very amused at the three Americans. He was an *abogado,* a lawyer, a word I recognized from signs in tenement windows on Manhattan's Upper West Side. He lived half time in Mar del Plata, a beach resort a few hours to the south, and the other half in Buenos Aires. He had just arrived here and instead of sitting home in his small pied-a-terre, decided to come out for a drink—of water. It was his first time at Titanic, but he had heard there were supposed to be dancers tonight.

"And where are the dancers?" I asked.

"I think they just went home with your friend," he joked.

My Golden Cadillac was gone and Ricky asked if I wanted another. "One Caddy's my limit," I said and, although he spoke English, it didn't translate. I offered Marcelo another water, but he declined.

*"La cuenta, por favor,"* I asked.

"No, it's all paid," Ricky said. "Your friends pay."

*Yes, probably with my fifty pesos,* I thought. "Great," I smiled, and with his gleaming white collar he danced off to another customer.

I twisted back to Marcelo who sat watching me. *Now what?* I thought.

"So what's churning in that dirty little brain of yours?" I said in English. He tipped his head like a puppy, not comprehending. He started doodling on my knee. He wanted to know where I was staying.

"A hotel, but I don't think I can bring anybody back there."

"No, no," he backpedaled, he was just wondering if we could take a taxi together. I guess I had made assumptions I shouldn't have.

"My flat is a mess, I just returned after a week away, but can I invite you back there, if you want?" Maybe I wasn't making assumptions after all.

"Well, sure…*si, bueno.*" It was one of my goals in coming to Buenos Aires—to be invited into someone's home or apartment so I could get an intimate look at how the natives lived here. It's like looking into someone's medicine chest in the bathroom when you're invited to a dinner party. This was my opportunity. Besides, he looked adorable. I tried appearing coy as I stepped down off the bar stool, which suddenly tipped off balance thrusting me toward him. Marcelo caught me as he too tipped backward. A couple of guys nearby who had been watching us reached out and grabbed us both. A cheer erupted when we were saved but the stools toppled. They patted our heads and rubbed our backs like we were all on a soccer team. Then they heightened the spectacle and thrust us together. Marcelo laughed like the groom at a wedding. He wrapped his arms around me and kissed me. Then he kissed me again, then deeper, then again even longer with a strong embrace. I shut out all the commotion around us.

*Okay, show me the way to your place,* I thought.

When we emerged onto the yellow artificial light of Avenida Callao he insisted we stop at an all night tobacco stand to buy some *preservativos.* Luckily from my Italian I knew that meant condoms and not what they add to food. He looked surprisingly more three-dimensional now that we were outside. I recognized for the first time that Marcelo was half a head shorter than I am. The gruff man behind the stacks of gum asked what type he wanted, holding up two different boxes. Marcelo turned to me for my opinion, as though we were buying a new lampshade. I had no idea what the difference was, so I pointed to the box with the prettier design. He took it from the man to examine more closely.

"*Si, si,*" he said. Never wanting natives to suspect that I'm a foreigner, I thrust a bill folded lengthwise between two fingers towards the man, not knowing if it was enough or if change was due. He slid the bill into a box then fingered his dish for two coins, which he placed on the counter and went back to listening to his transistor radio. Hands in his pockets, Marcelo looked at me sideways. He held my eye for one second, as if weighing his final decision. We were in a freeze-frame. Then he strolled to the street to hail a cab. He told the driver an address in the Recoleta district while he reached for my hand on the seat.

* * * *

We made love very slowly in his white bed. We never opened the silver package of condoms because we never had time for intercourse. I came three times that night but we didn't wipe anything away. We held our bodies snug. We kissed languorously; our faces brushed and snuggled. His tongue was like electricity and ice at the same time on my arms, my knees. My nipples erupted, scarlet with his touch. I licked his stomach, his chest, his thighs, and every crease I found. He smelled so sweet. I never noticed before how different the scent of a neck was from the scent of a back. We talked and whispered, no longer groping for words. His voice was like balm. He breathed on my face and blew a stream of air up and down my sides until goose flesh arose then hugged me to warm it away. We nuzzled more, just floating on the bed. We made love with the windows open, a silky breeze wrapping and rewrapping us all night. Sometimes his soft touch mimicked the breeze on my skin as we hugged. We spoke with our hands, our tongues, and our eyes. I rocked him in my arms while kissing his neck and smelling his springy black hair. We dozed, but never longer than ten minutes, sometimes together, sometimes separately. We explored ways to melt further into each other, his dead weight on top of me when he slept, his strong squeeze when he exhaled, his panting in my ear after glazing me with sperm.

In the breaking morning light Marcelo was not just adorable, he was beautiful. I watched his abdomen rise and fall peacefully. I watched him slide from sleep to awake so smoothly. I could only smile when his eyes looked directly at mine. I could see inside his Coca-Cola irises. Even with almost no sleep he sparkled. We lay side by side just looking while the light grew on us slowly but surely—the same way we had made love.

I felt so comfortable with Marcelo. The air around us was effervescent. I felt more like myself than I had in ages—4,000 miles from home. As he called me a taxi so I could meet my friends for our scheduled trip up north to Iguazú Falls I secretly studied his feet. I watched his hands hang up the telephone. I saw his curls bounce as he turned his head to me. The intimacy of the night hadn't changed. The passion wasn't spent. We stood holding hands, looking at each other for the full fifteen minutes it took for the cab to arrive. Breath in, breath out. Static electricity filled the synapse between us. He slipped on a tiny pair of gym shorts and walked me down to the black and yellow Radio Taxi outside. He was barefoot. The street was bustling. Everyone would know we had spent the night together. I was proud. Ducking his head inside the cab, he made sure the driver knew where I was going. Then he pulled me to his chest and kissed me in the warm sun. He touched my face as I lowered myself, dazed, into the backseat.

* * * *

The trip to Iguazú, way in the northeastern corner of Argentina, lasted two days. The falls were impressive, bigger than Niagara, but that last kiss rocked me more than all the pounding water. I couldn't wait to see Marcelo again—if only to verify that he was real. I called him as soon as our rickety plane touched ground. We repeated the first night. We repeated it three more times before I left Argentina. We had dinner together, I met him for lunch, we walked through neighborhoods so I could get a feel for the different parts of his city. We even took a tango lesson together in San Telmo. Marcelo and I were together every possible moment, and we learned to speak some combination of languages and signs that allowed us to discuss our lives, our work, family histories, dreams. I met his mother. I learned about the house he planned to build near the mountains. I suggested a design for the garden. He spent time with my friends, took us on a bicycle tour along the harbor, told us the story of how his father became one of "the disappeared"—those unfortunates on the wrong side of the military dictatorship's ideology, nabbed on the streets and never heard from again. The list of things we didn't have time to do together is long. What I felt for Marcelo in those few days was completely new to me, yet there was a surprising tranquility whenever we were together.

$*$ $*$ $*$ $*$

Our stay in Argentina was only one week, but it seemed like months since we had left New York. On Saturday I called Marcelo from the airport, at the last moment before our plane boarded. I wasn't going to, but I found myself swiping my American Express card in the airport telephone and punching in his number. I was shaking. We had already said farewell earlier that day. I didn't want him to come to the airport because I hate emotional good-byes. I've always preferred to just slip away. But I didn't know when I would hear his voice again. We laughed a little, nervously, but I was so sad that my heart was sinking into my intestines.

"Michael . . .," he began. Then he cleared his throat. "Michael," he repeated. And then the first sentence in English he had ever used: "I love you."

The tears that were barricaded behind my eyes fell. I never cry. The tears cascaded down my cheeks collecting around my chin. I couldn't speak. He thought I was gone.

"Michael? Michael?" he called. I sniffled to let him know I was still there. The phone was shaking in my hand.

"Oh, Marcelo, oh..." and I put my head against the phone and cried. He knew I was there. He heard me. He kept talking to me, his voice like balm, but all I could do was quiver. The boys came up to get me because the last call for boarding had passed. I could only whisper into the receiver, "Good-bye *mi amor,* adios." I hung up. Dennis put his arms around me and I sobbed into his shoulder. I couldn't catch my breath. No sound came out of my throat. He held me tight and didn't speak. When I took a breath, he coaxed me toward the gate.

I guess Steven picked up my bag. I don't remember getting onto the plane.

# ❧ 7

# Costumes, Customs, and One Camaro

*Ken Baehr*

Pulling the strap down across my chest, I fasten my seat belt. Scott doesn't care how fast he drives, so long as he speeds, his white Camaro racing toward Canada. Scott isn't too sensitive about most anything from what I've witnessed during the few months we've worked together at Crème de la Crème, the pastry café where we both wait tables. His favorite catchphrase is an exasperated "Don't flatter yourself," spoken with a practiced batting of the eyelashes. He's forever tan, with bright blue eyes, spiky blonde hair, and a menacing smile. But he could never be described as cool. Cool is something that gets in his way, like swizzle sticks, pedestrians, or the less confident. One drunken night I witnessed him butting out a cigarette on a guy's forehead over what appeared to be the location of an ashtray. This is a guy who always does as he pleases.

Scott changes lanes and music simultaneously. "Perfect," he snaps, as "(Every Day Is) Halloween" explodes out of the rear speakers. He reaches into the pocket of his denim jacket and pulls out a shiny green box of smokes, Dunhills.

I stare out the car window, watching the blur of landscape embanking Lake Ontario. The sinister dance music feeds my festive mood. I love Halloween, and this year would be better than most. It was Scott's idea to take off from work and drive to Toronto. Once there we'd buy some costumes and party until Sunday morning.

Scott suddenly hands me a freshly lit joint. *Why are we friends?* I think as I inhale slowly, deeply. Maybe he's drawn to my quiet confidence. Or my patience with him. We don't really have much more in common than work and being gay men in our early twenties. Sometimes that's just enough, I guess. After another contemplative puff, I pass him back the joint.

We're into Canada in no time, safely passing through the border check at Niagara Falls. It's 1992, still a decade away from the scrutiny borne of new-millennium terrorism. Road trips are still simple pleasures, lacking the sophistication of satellite radio, cell phone conversations, and a myriad of yet-to-be-developed gadgets.

With Speed Racer Scott behind the wheel, Toronto shouldn't be much more than an hour away. We zip along the rugged coast of Lake Ontario, the rocky corner shared by New York and Ontario. The horizon over the lake resembles a long narrow sidewalk crack, separating two shades of autumnal gray.

As we near the city limits, I see the CN Tower beckoning to us, a steely erection poised towards heaven. We're just minutes away now, and it feels like we're being reeled in, the winding stretch of the Queen Elizabeth Way spooling into itself, and us with it.

We're soon downtown, clean and cosmopolitan, the quintessential postcard city. The Camaro is given rest in a parking lot near the corner of Wellesley and Church Streets, the gay hub of Toronto. We have yet to determine which club to bless with our Yankee presence, or where to sleep. It's agreed that if things get bad enough, we'll just nap in the car. But being such prepared and experienced party boys, we couldn't go wrong. We've both been here before, and we know where to eat, drink, and shop, that holiest trinity of consumer culture. Checking ourselves in the vanity mirrors, we venture out.

I beeline it for my favorite gay boy's clothing shop, Body Body Wear, on Church Street. It offers the latest in fleeting fashion and undersized clubby vestments. The salesperson there, Sheila, is a young, cosmically enhanced girl who enjoys critiquing dance music while she cleans auras. The video for Madonna's latest single, "Deeper and Deeper," pops on the small television screen in the showroom. "This video is really fun," she offers as she wipes the negative particles from my personal space. "But she's so off key it hurts." We laugh as the vocals warble from the speakers.

The music inspires me to shop for something risqué, playfully pro-vocative. I squeeze into some black knee-length biker shorts. Sheila hands me a black lycra lace-up vest with silver eyelets. "This will go great with your boots and the handcuffs." My costume is now com-plete: S&M bike messenger...I think.

Meanwhile, Scott adds a matching sleeveless shirt to his snug white jeans. He claims to be an angel. *More like a great white shark,* I muse. "You're a perfect angel, Scott."

"I know," he says wryly, bloodshot eyes glued to his reflection. The irony is lost on dear, cosmic Sheila.

Thanking Sheila for the professional flattery masquerading as help, Scott and I leave the shop fully costumed. We head back to the car to drop off our clothes and finish off the roach left over from our joint. Once again stoned, it's decided that if separated, we'll just leave a note on the windshield for the other.

Drowsed by the marijuana, we go to the corner coffee bar, Second Cup, a Church Street institution. There's a buzz of oncoming excite-ment inside. Holiday drag queens, young witches, the crew of the En-terprise (the Next Generation), and various cowboys, cops, and creatures fill the cappuccino-scented room. Scott and I sit with our coffees at a small table near the door, discussing our potential targets as night falls on All Hallows' Eve.

A well-built young man with curly black hair stands at the next ta-ble. He's shirtless, in tight blue jeans, with two inflatable female sex dolls strapped to either side of him. He turns around to face us, dark eyes and a charming smile.

"Hey, guys. Happy Halloween," he says enthusiastically. Rubber handcuffs dangle from one of the doll's pink plastic ankles.

"Happy Halloween," Scott returns, equally playful.

"Do you know what I am?" the man asks as I take note of his lean hairless torso.

"Uh . . . no. Tell us," I say. The pot and caffeine have quickened my curiosity.

"I'm Madonna's sex book."

We all laugh. The controversy that was Madonna's best-selling book, *Sex,* stood before us in partially human form, smelling of new vinyl and cologne, Calvin Klein's Obsession. Reaching one hand into the fabricated vagina in front of him, he extracts two rolls of Smarties, a fittingly clever choice for such a well concealed candy, and offers them to us.

"I like your handcuffs," he says, examining them. "They're real, eh?"

"They're real to me," I tease. "Say, Sex Book, can you tell us a good place to go out tonight? You know, cool techno, open late . . ."

"Everything should be good tonight. I'm going just across the street now. There's a fun crowd over there. Why don't you come over and say hello?"

I welcome the suggestion. Scott agrees it would be as good a place as any to start the night's festivities.

"Okay, well . . . see you later. By the way, I'm Robert," he smiles.

"I'm Ken. This is my friend, Scott." *I would love to add my own lengthy chapter to his costume.* "Nice to meet you, Robert. Thanks for the candy."

After coffee, Scott and I venture across the street, to Pegasus, a large billiard hall bar, already patron packed. We head straight to the bar and order a round. I take a quick glance around for Sex Book Robert. He's hard to miss, a meaty six foot center to his inflatable love sandwich. Before long he makes his way through the merry mix and joins us for a drink. Then another. Scott looks anxious. I know what's coming next.

"I think we should go to the club soon," he asserts.

"I'm having a good time here."

"I can see that," he adds, his tone matching the pungency of our gin gimlets.

"Some of my friends are going to Heaven soon," Robert interjects. "Why don't you guys come with us?" His plump red lips curl into a flirtatious smile. *Sure. I would follow those lips across the Canadian Rockies.*

The mock angel gives me a smug look, as if to say, "Heaven. How appropriate."

An hour later Scott and I find ourselves at one of Toronto's larger clubs, but not really together. While he cruises along the long halls and dimly lit walls I'm handcuffed to Robert, his inflatable cohorts now sleeping off their day-long orgy somewhere in the downstairs coat check. A few times Scott passes me on the dance floor and throws a dirty look my way. Even over the acidic bass line of "James Brown is Dead" I can still hear Scott's even more acidic thoughts: *"Don't flatter yourself."*

Once I've released my newly revised copy of *Sex* to go use the bathroom, Scott approaches me, sans halo. "What are you doing?" He puffs at his menthol, conjuring a young Bette Davis.

"What do you mean? I'm just hanging out . . . having fun," I slur.

He looks at me like I'm not only missing the point, but never knew there was any point to be had. "You don't have a clue how to party out of town," he jabs. "I'm going to the bar. Have your fun." Scott disappears into a pride of men. *Just what was I supposed to be doing?*

Robert steps out of the men's room and gently grabs my arm. "Do you want to go dance?"

He's reading my gin-spiked mind. "More than anything."

Several rounds and extended dance remixes later I've lost all track of time, and my compatriot. I realize we'd never set a meeting spot for inside the club. Robert helps me search the space for him. I survey the parade of passing foreheads for fresh cigarette burns, signs of the angel's passing, but it's useless. Scott's gone.

I explain to Robert the agreement we made to leave a note on the car, and ask him to walk me over to Wellesley. On our way out, we pick up his two deflated girlfriends. Robert and I flirt our way to the car lot. *Why can't I meet anyone this cool back home?* We reach the lot and I drunkenly try to pinpoint the parking space. I don't so much remember parking the car, but I do remember its location from when we finished the joint. The Camaro should be here. Exactly right here. "So where do you think your friend is?" Robert asks.

A chilly blend of night air and panic sobers me. "I have no idea," I sigh. "We didn't make overnight plans, so there's not even a number to reach him." Robert continues asking a line of questions in an effort to help me locate my friend, the Camaro, or anything at all which might be construed as part of my life. A choke of feckless answers spurt out of me in nervous staccato, like the sputtering of a stubborn car engine. "Uh . . . um . . . uh . . . hmm." A confused looking go-go pirate stares back at me from a sedan window's reflection: my distressed altered ego. Robert and I try to untangle the possibilities and come up with more nothing. This was Scott we were trying to locate. He, the great white sharkangel. There was no chance he'd come looking for me. I suddenly felt quite cold and breathless, not unlike the loveless ladies draped over Robert's arm.

"If you want you can stay over at my place," offers my unarmored knight.

*If I want?* Warmth and oxygen return to my limbs. *Could it be that Scott, by abandoning me, had done me this favor?* I want. Robert hails a cab and we're in front of his apartment in minutes. He welcomes me in quietly, explaining that he has a light sleeper for a roommate. As he opens his bedroom door, something stirs in the neighboring bedroom. A door opens, then immediately slams closed.

"I can't believe you! Bringing someone here! You're an asshole, Robby!" the young woman shouts from behind the door. Light sleeper? Perhaps. Light speaker? Hardly.

Robert pulls me into his bedroom, closing the door and locking us in. He explains to me that his roommate hasn't yet gotten over her romantic feelings for him enough to accept his homosexuality. I nod, pretending this is just some commercial for a Canadian soap opera airing tomorrow, then quickly refocus my attention on the late-night erotic movie beginning tonight.

A first kiss. Then another.

Robert chooses a mix tape, less for atmosphere and more for drowning out the sounds of our private Halloween after party. The two inseparable party girls huddle in the corner, clinging to each other like shriveled shipwreck survivors, staring at us wide-eyed, unblinking, their red mouths agape in shock, as if they were privy to some rare and ritualist mating act by the island natives.

Music from the clothing store plays through my head. Robert and I spend the next several hours passionately reenacting scenes from Madonna's book. This would be some of the best "literature" I have ever known.

Finally, we sleep.

\* \* \* \*

It was one of those rare mornings when you should feel hungover but instead feel marvelously fresh and rested. Really good sex can do that, the heat of desire burning away the toxins in one's system. Fortunately for us, the soap opera damsel has made an early departure and we are left alone in the apartment.

"She'll be back tonight to give me hell," says my new friend.

I apologize for losing my ride back to America and for disrupting his home life, although I'm not really sorry. In fact, I'm quite pleased with how things have turned out. I don't like flashy sports cars anyway, I decide.

Having worked up lumberjacks' appetites, my host suggests we have brunch at a nearby café. I love this idea, except that my only clothes are a smelly lump of biker shorts and a scant pirate's vest on his bedroom floor. So, after we both shower, I'm outfitted with a T-shirt and some blue and white striped overalls, speckled with sea green paint that matches the bedroom walls. It's comfortable enough and the overalls look cool with my boots. One of the buckles is missing on the overalls, leaving one strap to dangle. It makes me feel like some character from a Mark Twain story, that is if he'd had written homoerotic fiction. Anagrams of Huck Finn quickly come to my mind.

The day is sunny, crisp, and cool, weather southern Canadians must take pride in. Robert mentions that he likes people with a lot of energy and ambition. He says I seem ambitious. In matters of the heart he's got me pegged. Red and yellow maple leaves cling to our boots, awakened from the dewy ground beneath us. Our arms rub against each other as we stroll, and I take in the scent of his clean wet hair drying in the autumn air.

Inside the oak-paneled café we sit by the front window and order two coffees. Pretending to read the brunch menu, I let my mind wander. *Will I ever see Robert again or was this nothing more than an over-the-border trick? A single night's piece of ass candy dropped into my tourist treat bag?* I look out the window to see a red streetcar passing by. My time here is nearly up.

We eat slowly, savoring the pancakes and sausages sweetened by maple syrup. Savoring too the night that was then, and the day that is now. I never felt like this before. *Why was I so enamored? Was it his dark exotic looks? His sexual prowess? Good humor? Or simply the fact that he thought to hide Smarties in the cavity of a sex doll he wore out in public? No, it wasn't that.* I didn't know the reason. I did know that I wanted to see him again, needed to. I relish in the thought that I'm wearing his clothes.

I put it out there. "I'm having such a good time. With you."

"I am too," he smiles, a sticky dab of syrup in the corner of mouth. "Give me your number so we can stay in touch, eh?"

*I love Canada.*

It's a short taxi trip to the bus terminal downtown. I'm beginning to feel tired and drained from the excitement, physical and otherwise. We walk to the ticket window where I pay for a one-way fare. There's only enough time to get to the gate. It's for the best anyway.

"Thanks for . . . everything," I say, limiting myself.

"It's my pleasure." We embrace for the first time without alcohol or costumes or sex. Just bodies sharing a moment. "Let's definitely keep in touch," he adds. "Okay?"

The bus is warm and ready to leave.

"Definitely."

One more hug. Shorter. Stronger.

I climb aboard and find a seat toward the back, hoping to sleep. Through the dirty window I smile out at Robert. He waves, also smiling. *Is it him that I don't want to leave or some moment in my life he might represent?* We pull out of the dark bus garage and into the bright streets of Toronto. Life feels fuller here, I think, new and promising. I've never failed or fumbled here in this taller, cleaner city of his.

I had only recently left my last boyfriend, who was also my first. We lived together for less than a year. He was incapable of loving me it seemed, so he would supplement for that handicap with control. There were verbal attacks, and a couple of physical episodes. Feeling helpless, I got up and left one day. I moved in with some friends who rented a spacious four bedroom house. My life opened up from then on. I had a newfound happiness that I now wanted to share with someone.

As the bus rolls slowly through a long tunnel I begin replaying the last twenty-four hours in my mind. It's like a news event the media won't let rest. Images reappearing. Sound bytes embedding themselves in my consciousness. "Deeper and Deeper" repeated in my head. "Round and round and round you go, when you find love you'll always know." I wanted to be with him, him with me. Although we would only be three hours apart by wheel, nurturing any sort of romance seemed unlikely. I'm working my way through college in my country while he's a struggling actor in his. These considerations don't discourage me, but neither are they reassuring.

Ninety minutes of hitting "mental replay" later, the bus pulls into the parking area for the border crossing. Every passenger gets off and lines up inside the small tidy customs office with any personal items they are transporting. I stand silently in line wondering what type of ordeal awaits me inside the questioning area. I have no passport, no driver's license, not even a library card. I have neither a wallet, nor any luggage. Any trace of my identity is somewhere in the trunk of a white Camaro. I have only my unshaven self, in paint-stained, pin-striped overalls and T-shirt, with a shiny set of dangling handcuffs. Not suspicious looking in the least. Even the most experienced border officials surely hadn't seen the likes of me before. If Scott only knew, he would be laughing his pot-filled head off over this one.

"Next in line."

I step up, looking like a gay, oversexed version of *The Fugitive*.

A middle-aged woman with glasses sits behind the counter, staring out at me. "Identification, please."

I'm at a total loss.

"What is your citizenship, sir?"

"American."

She asks me where I live and what I do for a living. She asks questions about the length and purpose of my stay in Canada.

I proceed to give her the condensed, made-for-family-viewing version of my costume, and subsequent abandonment. I feel a need to somehow explain these steely handcuffs.

She blinks, then asks "Who was the first president of the United States?"

"George Washington," I answer. *Doesn't everyone know that?*

"Can you recite the American pledge of allegiance?" she continues.

I think for a few seconds. How did that one start? Back in high school we never recited the pledge. Our entire bleary-eyed homeroom just stood there each morning, listening to the daily drone of the pledge over the muffled intercom speaker. It's been a dozen years since I've actually quoted the lovely patriotic oath.

It suddenly comes to mind, as familiar as a nursery rhyme and just as meaningful. "I pledge allegiance to the flag of the United States of America and to the Republic for which it stands, one nation under God, indivisible, with liberty and justice for all."

· No further questions. I'm back on the bus and heading for home. Back to find Scott, my belongings, and some answers.

The next few days I'm on an emotional high. I try to get in touch with Scott, but he isn't answering his phone and there's no answering machine. I know I will see him at the café soon enough. Robert and I speak throughout the week. We enjoy long conversations, laughter enriched, innuendo fortified. There is a certain chemistry, but what we do with it has yet to be established. He invites me to come stay with him as soon as I can. I will leave in two weeks.

At the café, I gently glide a serrated knife edge through a sugar-powdered layer of baked meringue, trying carefully not to disrupt the delicate configuration of cake, whipped cream, and fresh berries. Meticulous in cake, reckless in love. A shadow crosses over the cake plate.

"Oh, there you are," the familiar voice swaggers. It could only be him. Scott acts as if we've been separated for a matter of mere minutes.

"I am?" I set the knife down. "What happened to you?"

"Oh, that. I couldn't find you so I left. You must have been with what's his name." Scott slips a chocolate mousse cup out of the display case and grabs a teaspoon.

I would love to dump this Viennese meringue torte onto his smug fake tan. "Right. I was with Robert," stating this like one who celebrity name-drops. "He let me stay at his place that night."

"Just one night?" Scott licks mousse off the spoon.

I should be thanking him, but instead I'm hoping for an apology. I shake my head, sliding the torte back into the case before tossing the knife into the sink. My frustration seems to please him immensely. He adds, "I put your stuff in the kitchen for you."

The rest of the day I watch the clock, plotting the all-night study sessions ahead of me. If I was going back to Toronto I wasn't about to take any text books with me.

The weeks pass not quickly enough and I find myself again on the bus. This time I'm fully dressed, with proper identification, and a backpack containing a change of clothes, a disc player, my music, and a few gifts. Rainwater trickles down the bus window. I put on some music and close my eyes. *What am I doing? Is this some new thing beginning for me, or is this just a diversion of my senses?* It doesn't matter. My heart spoke and I must now obey.

Robert and I spend a playful weekend shopping, dining out, and renting movies. One night as we watch *Thelma and Louise* I hand him a small gift bag. He extracts a pint-sized paint can full of liquid chocolate, and a small paint brush. He giggles excitedly. We immediately undress, freeing the artists beneath the pedestrian clothing. Funny, I still can't tell you which one is Louise and which is Thelma.

This begins a series of trips to Toronto over the next few months. After my first visit, the roommate situation had become unbearable and Robert moved out and into his own, more spacious apartment. There are many more dinners, movies, and shopping. We exchange Hanukkah gifts and Christmas presents. I meet his friends and his brother, even his mom. The more of his world I see, the more I like it. This new city enchants me and gives me renewed purpose. *Is the city a means for me to see Robert or is Robert a means for me to see the city?*

Things between us continue to improve with each visit. Robert and I grow closer and closer. I think about how and when I will relocate to Canada. I wonder how many of my credits will transfer to Canadian universities. I speak to one of Robert's friends who has moved here from Jamaica, asking her to explain the legal issues I would need to address. Things have gotten quite serious since our handcuffs first locked wrists.

\* \* \* \*

One late afternoon, I arrive at Robert's apartment. February 13, 1993, to be precise. He greets me at the door with fresh tangy kisses. He smells of Obsession and hair mousse. It feels so good to be back here.

Agreeing to stay in, we shop for dinner. Robert grills some steaks on his terrace while I roast new potatoes and prepare a salad. On the television an episode of *The Golden Girls* repeats from the living room separating us. Robert walks in with meat sizzling. "Oh, my gosh. I love Dorothy. I think she's so funny." I take the plate of juicy steaks from his hands. *What's happening? Who's life is this?* My head feels foggy. Maybe it's the gas from the oven.

I nod. "I like Sophia. She gets away with anything."

I think about what I've just said, remembering how I'm supposed to be watching my roommate's car while she's away, but instead took her keys and secretly drove to Robert's place. Technically I'm still watching it, I justify. *What's wrong with me?* I arrange a steak on each of our plates, pink-brown juices swirling.

"The potatoes smell great." He kisses me warmly on the back of my neck.

"Rosemary," I say. "Let's eat."

We carry our plates into the living room and sit down. Robert pours two glasses of wine, handing one to me. "I have this early audition tomorrow, so you can just sleep in and I'll be back by ten or so."

"Oh, okay," I smile, still dwelling on the car I might have stolen.

After dinner, dessert, and a candlelit bath, my lover and I take long silk neckties into the living room. We proceed to find numerous ways to bind and blindfold each other to and upon pieces of overturned furniture. We bring in select food items from the kitchen. Were this an art exhibit, our tableaux vivant would have titles like: "Upside down recliner with blindfolded man and ice cubes," or "Allegory of nude holding himself on coffee table with whipped cream and honey."

I wake the next morning to the smell of brewing coffee. I stumble into the hall and toward the living room, the furniture now fully intact. A bouquet of long-stemmed red roses tower over the coffee table. Next to it is a Valentine's card, and a small, gift-wrapped package. Robert steps out of the kitchen with a fresh pot of coffee, the per-fect picture of romance and companionship. Naturally, I requite with a panic charged outburst.

"What the hell is all this?" I rant. "I asked you not to do anything like this, but you did it anyway!" I feel the veins surfacing on my neck.

Robert falls back against the wall, shocked, slowly deflating like his plastic friends who had introduced us. Tears spill down the face that only seconds ago was full of joy and levity.

I let my monster continue. "That's it! I'm leaving. I can't do this anymore." I ramble on madly. "I'm sorry, but I really have to go."

I march into the bedroom and start dressing. I'm still packed from just arriving the day before. I can hear crying from the next room. I tell myself it's just theatrics. He's an actor. Not to let it bother me. *My God, what is the matter with me?*

I'm out the door minutes later, leaving only apologies behind, apol-ogies and a gift unopened, a card unread. At the car, I brush the thin layer of snow off the windshield, my hand trembling in its black glove. I unlock the door, climb inside and turn the ignition. The little red Honda moans without starting. I've disrespected it as well, I know. I pray for it to start. Getting stranded here twice would be too cruel, yet after what I had just done not completely undeserved. I try again. With a wheeze, it struggles harder to start. It's barely running.

Normally I would let the car warm up. It is the middle of February, but there's no time to do what's right. I need to be back home, in a life that's wholly recognizable, secure in its narrowness. I wasn't ready for love, to be subjected to its honesty and omnipotence. I couldn't yet re-linquish the reigns of my feelings and confess knowingly that amor vincit omnia. I steer the old Honda out on to the street and press down on the accelerator. The cold car shakes, like Robert had just mo-ments ago, crying into his hands. *Just get me home.*

As I drive away from Toronto, I spy the CN Tower in my rearview mirror, now seeming like a tall shameful finger, commanding me to exit. I imagine myself looking out from its lofty observation deck, see-ing the world with a bigger view, with new eyes. I suddenly understand that I'm in need of something larger than what I'm experiencing in my life, but not love, and not Toronto. I decide that it's time for me to move, to New York City. I click on the radio and turn onto the QEW.

# 8

# Paradox

*Thomas Bradbury*

"I can't get on my flight," I said into the cell phone.

"Why not?" Askin said.

"I made a big mistake. I booked the flight but I never got the tickets and the airline cancelled my reservations and now the flight is sold out."

I was nervous, thinking he was about to read me the riot act but instead he just said, "Oh."

This was a particularly humiliating situation for me because I am a travel agent. I am like the cobbler's son who has no shoes. How could I have made such a stupid mistake? Now, I had to think. How was I going to get to Askin? I only had three days for this trip and I needed to see him.

Askin and I had been apart for almost four months and I longed to see him. The airport in Istanbul was packed with people stranded and many of them were at the standby counter with me trying to get on fully booked flights.

"Listen, I think I can get on a flight to Antalya and I will rent a car and drive down." He hesitated. He rarely told me not to do anything, but I waited.

"Okay, be care," he said making a grammatical error.

I wasn't particularly thrilled with the idea of having to drive three and a half hours at night but I really didn't want to wait. The flight the next morning was sold out as well. I was about to do something I told my clients never to do—drive at night in Turkey.

I called my business partner, Seren, and told her what I was doing. Could she get me a car in Antalya that I would drop off in Dalaman on Sunday? She called back. All the car companies in Antalya were sold out except Hertz, and they wanted 100 million lira a day and 95 euro drop fee. It was going to cost me as much to get to him as it had cost me to fly from New York to Istanbul. What should I do? It was too much. Maybe I should just spend the night in Antalya and take the bus down the next day.

Seren reasoned with me. "You don't want to do that. Listen, just take the car and go."

"Okay, but listen I think there is a shortcut down. Can you call Hasan (our local agent in Kas) and ask him for directions on that road and call me back?" She said she would do that and get back to me.

Upon arrival in Antalya, with a new Ford Fiesta from Hertz and directions from Hasan, I began my drive, through the mountains, in Turkey, at night. This is a particularly dangerous because Turkey is notorious for having trucks, tractors, scooters, and even horse-drawn wagons on their highways at night without lights. You think you are on a road by yourself doing 120 kilometers an hour and suddenly come upon an apparition doing 20. I took a deep breath, told myself to stay alert, and got going.

Two hours later, my cell phone rang. "Where are you?"

"I am outside Demre."

"One and a half hours later, you are here."

"Okay, I will call you when I am closer."

An hour later my cell phone rings again. This time more urgently, he asks, "Where are you?"

"I am in Fethiye."

"Half hour later now."

Sometime later another call, this time angrily, "Where are you?"

"Askin, I am almost there."

"Ha," he says, hanging up on me.

Arriving at his house, I am concentrating on parking as he suddenly appears beside the car. He startles me at first, but then I see the big smile on his face. He had grown a mustache and goatee since the last time I saw him. I wondered where he'd gotten the idea for this new modern western style, but it suited him. He shook my hand and kissed me on both cheeks, the traditional Turkish greeting. This is for the benefit of watching neighbors. And they were always watching.

\* \* \* \*

Askin and I had met ten years earlier on my first trip to Turkey. I had booked into a small hotel on the Mediterranean. It was late when I arrived and I asked at the desk if I could still eat something. The clerk said that I could, and he led me to the hotel's restaurant. I was the only one there and he became my waiter. After my meal he asked if I wanted to finish my wine in the bar.

The bar was done in Anatolian style, with cushions on the floor and the walls covered in Turkish carpets and fabrics. He sat down next to me and started to talk to me. His English was limited, my Turkish nonexistent. Out of nowhere he suddenly leaned over and kissed me. He said, "Go to your room, I will be there in an hour." It was two days before Christmas, and I felt like I'd just been given a very special gift. I spent five days in that hotel—three days longer than I'd expected. Every chance he got he'd visit me in my room. It was my best Christmas ever.

When I returned to New York, I looked back on our time together as simply a vacation fling, but one day I had a sudden urge to call him. When I called the hotel, he was the one who answered.

"I have not been happy since you left," he told me.

I immediately made plans to go back and see him in a month. He told me it would not be good for him to meet me there and that we should meet in a larger city. He said if his brothers found out about us they would kill him.

So began a pattern. We would always meet away from his hometown. On some occasions there were things that would happen that would leave me wondering, but I would always assume they had to do with our cultural differences. Our first fight happened when we were sitting talking with a group of boys at a small pension in Antalya. Askin said something that I knew was patently untrue and as I was just learning Turkish, I jokingly said *"yalanci,"* (liar) to him. He got up immediately from the table and went storming off to our room.

When I would call him at home I would hear children in the background. When I asked about it, he simply explained that he lived with his sister and her children. Her husband was off working in Hopa on the Georgian border.

I was excited the first time we were going to Istanbul together. In a cosmopolitan city like that I thought we could be more comfortable and he would be more open. As a surprise, I decided to take him to a very nice gay bar I knew there. It was on the top floor of a building, with a beautiful 360-degree view of the Bosphorus. Askin took one look around and fled. I chased after him, asking what was the matter, but he just kept walking. When we got back to our hotel room he turned and looked at me and said, "I am not gay."

I was incredulous. "What are you talking about?" We had been in bed together not more than a few hours earlier.

"I am not gay," he replied. "I like gay people, I like to look at gay people, but I am not gay." I was completely befuddled but didn't know what to say in response to him. On our next trip to Istanbul, he asked me to take him to a gay bar.

On another trip to Antalya, a Dutch woman friend, who was married to a Turk, told me, "Look, this is a village man. His family is going to expect him to get married. He will have to marry someday. It isn't so much that he is with you but his family will force him to marry. To not marry in a village is just not done." I remembered how once we had met a friend of his in a restaurant. His friend asked if I was married, and when I said no he appeared visibly shocked. Later when I asked Askin why his friend had reacted like that he answered with typical Turkish bluntness, "Because you are old." (I was forty.)

Later that night, when we were in bed together, I asked him, "Is this true what Emmy told me? Will you have to marry someday?" He answered that yes, he would.

"The day you get married is the last day we are together," I told him.

He was very moody for a long time after that, but then one day, suddenly, everything changed. I asked him what had caused the improvement. He told me it was because he had decided not to marry. I was happy.

After a couple of years of long distance commuting I decided to take a leave of absence from my job to spend six months in Turkey. I wanted to know if we could make a go of it together. We had been unsuccessful in getting him an American visa, so I thought I would just move there. When I told him my plan he was less than enthusiastic but he wouldn't tell me not to come. He was between jobs and I said we could travel in Turkey together and see if we could find someplace to live in his country, someplace where we could both be comfortable together.

When I got there, he met me in Antalya and we spent a week together. He said he had to go home to take care of some business and he would meet me in Bodrum in a week. Yet, when I got there, he didn't show up. I started calling his house.

The woman who answered the phone said he was working and she couldn't reach him either. I was worried but I also knew that this was Turkey and this is the kind of thing that happened here. When I finally reached him he said he had to take a job and they didn't have a phone where he was working but he would try to join me in Bozcaada in a week. When I got to Bozcaada he said he couldn't come. In the meantime, another Turkish friend had joined me on my travels, and since we were having quite a good time traveling together I decided to ignore my problems with Askin for the time being.

Askin continued to put me off. I decided to go to his village and find out for myself what was going on. I was furious with him. I didn't approach him directly because I didn't want to put him in harm's way, but I did want to talk to him and find out what was going on. I thought maybe our affair had run its course. It wouldn't have been the first time. I was so frustrated and confused by everything that had happened that I finally confessed my affair to a young American woman working in the hotel where I was staying. She had lived in Turkey far longer than me. Affairs between foreigners and Turks are nothing out of the ordinary and I thought she might be able to decipher the mysteries of my relationship. A couple of days later she said, "I have to tell you something that Tom from the travel agency said to me the other day. He said, 'You should see Askin's two sons. They are the most adorable children I have ever seen.'"

I said, "Oh no, those aren't his children, they're his nephews, his sister's children."

"I don't think so," she answered.

I decided to get to the bottom of this. I knew one of the other men who worked in the hotel was related to him and the next morning I screwed up the courage and asked him in Turkish.

"Do you remember, Askin, who used to work here? Is he married?"

He said, "Oh yes, he is my *Abi*. [literally older brother, but in this case his older cousin]. He has two boys."

I was sick at heart. I went downstairs and called my friend Emmy. "Askin is married. I am leaving and never seeing him again. It's over."

Emmy counseled, "Of course it's over. It has to be, but I know that he loves you and you must go and talk to him.

The next morning I went to where he was working. I knew he would be alone. We went in the back and sat down. I blurted out, "I know you are married!"

He burst into tears. "Who told you?"

"Why didn't you tell me?" I demanded.

"You said if I was married we were finished." I remembered my ultimatum. He said, "Please come back at noon and I will take you to meet my family."

I decided I had nothing to lose. It was over and I might as well meet them. I was curious.

As we were driving to his house he told me he had married when he was very young, only seventeen. His wife was from his small village and it had been an arranged marriage.

She was a very good woman and he loved her like a sister. When I arrived at their house I gave his wife a present I had brought, some Turkish pottery. In the traditional Turkish way she put it to one side and didn't open it in front of me. The boys were truly adorable, and they were all over Askin, kissing and hugging him. The littlest one, five at the time, hung on him. They brought out photo albums of the family and showed me pictures of the older one's *sunnet*, the traditional Muslim circumcision. I was a little shocked that they even had pictures of the boy's penis after the operation. Surprising in a country of great modesty.

After having tea, Askin said we should drive to his family vineyard and meet his father and mother, a half hour away. The father had lived in Germany for many years as a pharmacist and was very frustrated that as a foreigner I could not speak German. Askin barbecued some meat and we ate on the floor in the typical Anatolian way.

As we were leaving the father said to me, "Don't forget us."

\* \* \* \*

Over the years, I had resolved many times to break it off with Askin. Once I went so far as to say to him, "Listen, this isn't working. Let's stop."

He answered, "No, we have been together this long. I am not breaking up with you!"

We have been together for almost ten years now. It has been said that I am a commuter to Turkey. I am not sure why the relationship has lasted. The cultural differences make it possible and the fact that it is a long-distance relationship may keep it going. It hasn't been smooth sailing, and there are many times when it feels too hard, but then there are moments of intense satisfaction.

So now I am back and he is taking the luggage into the house. At the door his wife, Anet, is waiting for me.

"*Hos geldin, Abi,*" she greets me warmly. (Welcome older brother.)

"*Hos bulduk, Anet,*" I reply. (It is good to see you.)

As I sit down on the couch, the youngest one comes running out of his bedroom, eyes just barely open, sleep all over his face.

"*Amca,*" he whispers (Uncle.) He climbs up into my lap and wraps his arms tightly around my neck.

I feel content. Reunited with my lover, holding his child in my arms. Anet enters with the tea. I am home.

# 9

# Samoa Memories

*M. S. Hunter*

It is nearly a half century now since the U.S. Office of Territories sent me to American Samoa on temporary duty as counsel to the Samoan legislature during its annual session. I had been dealing with Samoan affairs in the Department of the Interior for over a year, and I had even made an effort to learn the basics of the Samoan language. In college I had, of course, read Margaret Mead's anthropology classic *Coming of Age in Samoa,* a book describing a culture wherein young men and women enjoyed complete sexual license and indulged in widespread promiscuity until marriage. So I knew what to expect. Right?

Wrong!

In those days there was no tourism and no hotels in American Samoa. No one was allowed to set foot there without specific authorization from the territorial government. So when the Pan Am flight from Hawaii to Australia landed at Tutuila, American Samoa's main island, I was the only non-Samoan to debark. I was greeted by the territorial attorney general, an American, and driven to the capital, Fagatago, in the governor's limo. The driver was a Samoan police sergeant. While chatting with the AG I admired the scenery—not so much the sparkling blue waters of Pago Pago Bay and the jungle-clad slopes of Mount Rainmaker as the lovely young Samoan men all along the road. Clad in nothing but colorful *lavalavas* wrapped around their waists, they revealed smooth, muscular, golden torsos crowned by handsome Polynesian features. I firmly reminded myself that I was there as a government official, a VIP, and that I could spend the next month looking but not touching.

*Looking for Love in Faraway Places*
doi:10.1300/5366_09

Once deposited at the furnished apartment provided for my use, I was at loose ends until a cocktail party at Government House that evening. So I set out on a walking tour to explore the village. I hadn't gone far when a car pulled up beside me—the governor's limo with the same police sergeant, the governor's chauffeur, at the wheel. "Where you going?" he asked.

"Oh, just for a walk."

"Hop in. I'll drive you around."

I did, and he did, ending at a little hillside bar where we drank a couple of beers. The conversation was innocuous, and finally I told him I had to get back to clean up and get ready for the governor's party. He drove me back to the apartment but, instead of just dropping me off, he followed me inside. I told him to make himself comfortable while I went through the bedroom and into the bathroom for my shower.

When I emerged from the shower he was standing in the bedroom by the bathroom door. He immediately grabbed me. I couldn't have been more surprised or shocked if it had been rape. But I can't use that word since, once his intentions were clear, I willingly let him have his wicked way with me. When it was over and we were dressing I said, "That was a surprise. Isn't that very unusual behavior for Samoan men? I didn't think they went in for that sort of thing."

"Oh yes," he said. "Very unusual."

Liar!

The next afternoon I was sitting at a booth in the Pago Bar, a big barnlike beer hall right on the village green, in the center of Fagatago and right next door to the building where the legislature met and where I had my office. The bar was nearly empty at that hour. My companions were two older Samoans, the chief who had been assigned to me as my translator and assistant and the Speaker of the House of Representatives. A little waitress minced over to take our orders—beer, of course, as nothing stronger was served there. She wore her *lavalava* tucked up like a miniskirt and a short-sleeved shirt tied at the bottom to make a halter. As she left our table I remarked in my best butch, one-of-the-boys voice, "Boy! She sure is flat chested."

My companions roared with laughter. "That's not a girl," I was informed. "That's a *fa'a fa'ine!*"

I did a double take. *"Fa'a"* I knew meant "like" or "in the manner of," as in *"fa'a* Samoa," according to Samoan custom. *"Fa'ine"* I knew was the word for girl or woman. In short I'd just been told that our "waitress" was a little drag queen. Looking around the room I realized that the entire waitstaff of the Pago Bar consisted of *fa'a fa'ines*. Now why didn't Margaret Mead ever tell us about Samoan *fa'a fa'ines?*

I returned alone to the Pago Bar that night. It was full with, as nearly as I could tell, an exclusively male crowd. I took a table by myself at the front and ordered a beer. Later I walked back to the men's room. On my return I passed a table with half a dozen young men who called out to me and invited me to join them. "Come! Sit with us," one shouted. I accepted, went back to my table, recovered my beer, and sat down with them.

"Where you from?" I was asked.

"The United States."

"And where your wife? She with you?"

"No. I'm single."

The words were hardly out of my mouth when broad grins appeared on my companions' faces, six bare feet landed on my feet under the table, and they practically chorused, "We single too!" Needless to say that was the beginning of an interesting evening.

After many more rounds of beer—the Samoans are the greatest beer drinkers I've ever encountered, with the possible exception of the Aleuts of the Pribilof Islands in the Bering Sea—we piled into a pickup truck and drove to a lonely area of bushes near the airport runway. It was there I learned that few young Samoans wear underwear beneath their *lavalavas*.

I will not attempt to recount all my amorous adventures in that paradise. The young men with whom I was intimate covered the entire range of Samoan society. There were boxers, students, sailors, the son of a senator, the youngest member of the legislature, port policemen, and many others. I met them everywhere—the Pago Bar and other bars, strolling about at night, or even in the day, and even at work in the legislature. The venues for our carnal romps ranged from

Samoan *fales,* or open-air community halls, to the beaches, the belfry of a church steeple, the wild bushy places, and, rarely, my own bed.

Those young Samoans were undoubtedly attractive, unless you prefer bears. That is, until their late twenties when, regrettably, and with few exceptions, they can become quite fat. A steady diet of taro is not recommended for maintaining a svelte figure. But before then their smooth, supple bodies and their passionate temperament made for memorable encounters. Nor were they least bit shy about letting you know what they wanted, and it wasn't always the same thing. Most were what is commonly called "versatile."

Just from looking out of my office window where I could see young men playing ball games on the village green was a delight. For this they hiked up the hems of their *lavalavas* and tucked them into their waists, creating a baggy pair of shorts. On more than one occasion I saw a tackle pull one of the impromptu shorts right off. Amid gales of laughter the boy's loins were promptly rewrapped, but not before I had been treated to the charming spectacle of brown buns and family jewels.

I spent one pleasant weekend in a village over the mountain on the north coast of Tutuila visiting the family of a young Senate page I had befriended. A cousin of his made the excursion memorable. It was in that village that I had a unique cultural experience. I was sitting cross-legged between the page and his cousin in the middle of a crowd of villagers under the thatched roof of an open-sided *fale.* In the distance beyond the shore I could see the moonlit Pacific. We were there watching the one village television set and the entertainment that night was the old black-and-white show, *Adventures in Paradise.* It was about the exploits of the captain of a beautiful white sailing vessel traveling around among the Polynesian islands. The background scenery was the same as that which surrounded us. The Samoans loved it!

Lest I give the wrong impression, my activities in Samoa were not all related to my erotic adventures. I did good work drafting bills for the legislature, explaining the significance and import of other bills to members of the Senate and House, and quietly but effectively promoting the governor's own legislative agenda. I even pushed through a couple of pet bills of my own, including one to ban roadside advertising. Billboards had yet to mar the beautiful Samoan landscape, and I was determined that they never would.

There were enjoyable times in this work, too. I went deep-sea fishing with influential senators. I attended *fia-fias* (parties) and pig roasts where I danced with the wives and daughters of legislators. I went on excursions to remote and lovely beaches with the government secretary (lieutenant governor) and his Samoan girlfriend. I shot pool with members of the legislature—the same pool table on which I had recently spent a night of erotic dalliance with the young man who managed the pool room.

By the time my day of departure from Samoa arrived I had reached the conclusion that it was wrong to say that Samoan boys were available and agreeable to gay sex. No, they were *eager* and *aggressive* in their pursuit of such relationships. Why was this so? I believe the explanation lies in the fact that the virginity of young women was valued and guarded there with an avidity that I have never known anyplace else. I do not know if this was the case before the conversion of the Samoans to Christianity, but that was a long while ago. Certainly the missionaries did a thorough job of convincing the Samoans that premarital sex for women was a serious sin. They did not, however, convince them—or perhaps they never really tried—that sex between males was equally sinful. As a result, deprived of a heterosexual outlet, the young men of Samoa freely, joyfully, and without apparent inhibitions, turned to one another. And I, as a young, single, and exotic foreigner was the fortunate beneficiary of that custom.

How did Margaret Mead get it all so very wrong? I learned the answer when I talked with some elderly Samoans from Manu'a, the island a few miles east of Tutuila where she did her field research. I asked them if they remembered Margaret Mead. That laughed and assured me that they remembered her well.

"We were boys then," they told me, "and she interviewed us. She asked about our sex lives and we told her all the dreams and fantasies we had about sex with the girls. The girls we knew heard about it and thought it very funny. So they told her the same stories. That silly white woman just wrote it all down." So much for *Coming of Age in Samoa!*

Would I find the same situation if I visited American Samoa today? I seriously doubt it. Shortly after my visit the first tourist hotel on Tutuila opened its doors and tourism with all its corrosive effects arrived on the island. It is unlikely that I could now sit drinking beer with a group of young Samoans and be told, as I was then, that I would not be allowed to buy a round of drinks because "you are our guest here in our country." And I would expect that those eager, ingenuous, completely nonmercenary boys have been replaced by a generation of young hustlers who have learned that gay tourists will pay to enjoy the pleasures of their bodies. Such are the inevitable "benefits" of tourism.

I would have happily returned to Samoa the next year if my assignment had been extended, but the opportunity did not arise. Now, after nearly half a century, I would not care to return there at all. Quite aside from the fact that I am no longer the sexy young stud that the Samoan boys pursued then, I know that other almost certain changes would dismay me. I have learned from disappointing return visits to other formerly favorite places that Thomas Wolfe was right when he told us we couldn't go home again.

# 10

# The Shosholoza Meyl:
# Johannesburg to Cape Town

*Des Ariel*

A brooding midday cloud looms over the flat inner veldt. In South Africa, I'm a little numb as I stare out at the land of the so-called "dark" continent, rich in gold, diamonds, and raw, psychic wounds. I am staring out of the window of the Shosholoza Meyl, a train that travels from Johannesburg to the Western Cape. It is hardly the luxury Blue Train with dress-for-champagne dinners, which is fully booked, but the Shosholoza Meyl has first and second class, and is within an average person's budget. It gets you to Cape Town just the same, removing you from the snarl that is central Johannesburg. The landscape that glides before my eyes is not just new terrain, but broken modes of myself writ large.

.The Shosholoza Meyl takes twenty-four hours, only few of which I gratefully slept through. For me it is a speeded-up epoch. I am not the same person I was in Pretoria, only a week before, having just been terminated by my South-African lover. I arrived, elated to meet him after three months of online courtesy, courtship, and growing anticipation; had one week of explosive passion in Pretoria; then it abruptly ended, like dismemberment. Weightless and disoriented I'm sucked inward. My life must move on like this damned train, but my heart pulls backward, sapping interest in the view. I glance reluctantly across terrain that may have inspired J. R. R. Tolkien—born in Bloemfontein—to create Middle-Earth. The dark fields are suddenly floodlit by a stark sun, and it's transformed into Mordor, and I am Frodo's ring in need of a meltdown.

### *"I'm just not feeling what you're feeling."*

Way past Kimberly we enter the Great Karoo region. Towns pass by: Scholtzkop, Hopetown, Drakenstein, Slanghoek, Noblesfontein, Elandskloof, and Beaufort West, names from an alien world. Like all train journeys we squander so much time wondering about what we've left behind and what's coming up that we miss the in-between stages, sometimes deliberately disregarding them. Few dare admit that traveling can be tedium packaged and sold in brochures as thrill after thrill. Why do we go to far-flung places where no one knows us?

In a field a lone ostrich is lost from its pack. Its legs are precarious stilts, but muscular. It looks stricken by fear, frantically twitching its long neck, back and forth. I wouldn't like to be the one obliged to catch it. A panicking ostrich has been known to simply kick humans to an ignominious death.

In the food car I make a desultory effort to eat. The waitress, smiling, but disgruntled, can't get a word out of me. She waits for me to say, "Thank you." But I mumble, mouth dry, wanting to explain but unable to. To her, passengers who don't chat much are scum. She waddles off, her black and orange head scarf tottering in a loose twirl on her head. Other waiters start talking to me in Afrikaans just because I'm white. White people are increasingly an irrelevance in South Africa. Novels by John Coetzee and Damon Galgut tell us that Western cultural tropes have little currency in post-apartheid South Africa. No one reads novels here, not even Alan Paton's *Cry, the Beloved Country,* which I bring to read. My Tswana lover, the one I came to meet, said, in a soft, pained voice, full of personal weariness I hear echoing, "I'm afraid of what books will tell me. So, I don't read them." In any case, knowing the name of Nobel Prize winner Nadine Gordimer doesn't put food on your plate in the townships or pay the rent, if you are lucky enough to get out.

Travel is a superior mode of introspection all right, especially on trains, where the internal conversation allows for fresh plasma of thoughts to be churned out. Such journeys occur due to a cry for change deep within, or because you are the outsider in your own backyard and you feel you belong somewhere else where people have the authentic values you find lost or lacking at home. The main action of travel is not external—it's all inside. The world out there is very cunning. It reflects the inner, and the landscape assumes the distorted hues of your microdrama, as when a shadow plows down across the hills, blotting out sunlight and adding menace to the scene. You think, yes, *that's* how I feel right now—the landscape's talking, inking in stuff you are otherwise unable to face.

Also, you are what you read. Rian Malan's book *My Traitor's Heart* says that 45 percent of South Africans believe that illness or misfortune results from "loss or damage" to the soul inflicted by witchcraft or wrathful "shades." In the rural areas that goes up to around 80 percent. A witch doctor (or *sangoma*) is needed to keep them at bay. In 1985, eighty four *sangoma*/sorcerers were burned or stoned to death in Johannesburg, a sign that even though Soweto's football teams all have a resident witchdoctor, casting bones to ensure success, some of the old white cultural values that sought to suppress them were not changing. Malan also mentions the *tokoloshe*, a mischievous nocturnal spirit. Africans sleep with their beds raised on bricks to avoid attack. In how much we believe, or how much we put aside as superstition, there is always an element from black Africans of pandering to white fears, and from white Africans or Europeans, wild assumptions about uneducated black beliefs. Black people tend to seduce white visitors with the stories they want to hear. Even so, I try to rest, and wonder whether my grandfather is looking down on me, disapproving. After all, the *tokoloshe* might feed on someone in just such a vulnerable mood during my jittery night's sleep.

### *"You're a nice guy, but I don't think this can go anywhere."*

A day later, in my guest house attic room in blustery Green Point, Cape Town, I switch on the TV, hoping for some distraction. But no. Instead, the names of murdered men are called out: Stephanus "Fanie" Fouché, 17; Travis Reade, 20; Marius Meyer, 21; Warren Visser, 21; Sergio De Castro, 22; Juan Meyer, 22; Timothy Greg Boyd, 29; Gregory Berghaus, 43; and Aubrey "Eric" Otgaar, 56. Names of victims, but not of culprits, yet. It's January 2003. This is the Sizzlers sauna massacre, fresh in the news. At the time, police believe four killers were hired from Johannesburg (called Jo'burg by locals) who may be members of the dreaded drug gang called the "Fast Guns." The killers are believed to be well built, with shaved heads, and possible snake tattoos on their arms—the type of murderer Jean Genet, were he alive, would make the totem of erotic adulation. South Africa is agog at the horror of these murders. Each victim forced to the floor, bound, gagged, throats slit, execution-style gunshot wounds to the back of the head. Then, abandoning the men for dead, the killers absconding with 2,000 rand in cash.

In a twisted way this bizarre killing helps me to put my own distress and dislocation into crooked perspective. Though the rejecting words I hear sting like bullets, and I'm staggering with wounds only I can feel and no one else cares about, I'm forced to think, *What kind of life is it that ends nasty, brutish, short, while the killers get away?* So I begin to fill my head with details of the murder.

The victims once worked at Sizzlers, 7 Graham Road, Sea Point— the seedier area of Cape Town—for about 120 rand a session, slightly less than twenty U.S. dollars. Many of the young men lived there. They used the escort business as a stepping stone to a more professional career, or just to pay off debts. Whether gay, straight, or undecided is not the burning issue, but male-to-male was definitely on the menu at Sizzlers. At the time, the papers said the only thing Eric, Mr. Otgaar, the owner, didn't tolerate was drugs. He spoke out in public about hard drugs, and warned his harem of boys of instant expulsion if they used them on the premises. Some believe this may have helped cut his life short.

### *"There's something I meant to tell you, but was afraid."*

In the early hours of Monday, January 20, 2003, an exhausted young man, Quinton Taylor, with blood pouring from gunshot wounds in the back of his head, totters into a gas station for help. His mates are all still crawling in their own blood. When the domestic, Ethel, turns up at the door and finds the police, the slaughtered staff, and Mr. Otgaar "Aubrey" dead, she goes to pieces. Two survivors of the gunshot wounds are taken to Groote Schurr hospital. Only Quinton is later able to identify the two killers.

There's always the possibility of homophobic motives for killings of gays. Most think not, yet gays and sex workers are often at risk. One trail of evidence lead to Mark Belcher, an escort who prefers to be known as a gigolo (i.e., he sometimes escorts for women too). He has flirted with Islam, reading the Koran enough to change his name to Maroewaan. He and his friend Stephen are thought to be the prey the killers wanted. That, and the 250,000 rand owed to them in a cocaine deal. As the theory goes, when the alleged killers couldn't find Maroewaan, who now is nervous of revealing more to the police, they killed the Sizzlers boys anyway. Mr. Belcher missed his own appointed death. This part fascinates me, as I came and missed my appointed love mate, and the connective tissue of circumstances never fails to amaze. More pain helps blot out pain.

Later, two men, Trevor Theys, a taxi driver, and Adam Woest, a waiter from Cape Town, are arrested and charged. A curious thing happens. The mother of Warren, one of the victims, who is a born-again Christian, visits Adam and shakes his hand as he languishes in prison. She nervously hands her son's murderer some toiletries, some clothing, and Warren's favorite Bible. She feels relieved. Quinton, the survivor, suggests that the murderers had helpers who are not coming forward. Adam and Trevor will take the rap in the trial, will eventually be sentenced to serve in prison nine consecutive life terms. My Twsana lover had wanted to take me to meet his mother. He wanted me to go into the townships, which I would have gladly done.

*"I want you to like my family.*
*I want you to be good to them please."*

It never happened, aborted before it could reach that legitimate "Mom, this is my lover" stage.

I can't watch or read the news anymore. Though still sore about being dumped, and concerned that murderers are still at large, I try to act as though on holiday still. I'm not fit company for a dinner party, yet Cape Town, I reason, still has much to offer. New sights and sounds can be a balm to battered esteem. So, I'm now standing on an almost perfect beach called Sandy Bay, famed for its nudist capers and hard cruising, though there aren't many people about. They are mainly white, though with respectable, hard-earned tans. Large rocks as smooth as the backs of elephants, bushes thrust upwards as far as Lion's Head rock, hot sun, crashing waves, a sense of freedom and sexual abandon. Here, I meet a guy who's mixed-race, tanned darker from sunbathing rather than natural color. He allows me to fumble with his dick, which is falling out of open shorts, but seems otherwise disinterested. Like many, he is too restless to settle for anyone—the search is everything. Later we meet again and chat as friends. After a day of skin being chafed by the winter sun, I decide to go back to the guest house. My new friend, whose name is Ahmed, accompanies me. He's a gardener from one of the Cape Flats shanty towns, a Muslim, one of the countless underclass of the Western Cape. As I climb the big boulders, push back the ferns, and continue up the hill to the road, he follows. Could he have a cigarette? I don't have any. He seems harmless. We pass the car watchmen who carries a long stick for beating off car thieves, and cadge a cigarette. We have to hitch as no buses leave from here. Ahmed says I must be the one to ask as not one of these men, all with nice cars and villas, will stop for a black.

Finally one guy stops. I ask him if it's okay for Ahmed to come too. The handsome driver looks doubtful, but is polite enough and nods okay. We pile into a smart, silver BMW. He's manager of a Web design company, just come back from the States. We exchange notes about New York for a while. I happen to mention the Sizzlers massacre, the prevailing dark mood. As we negotiate bend after hairpin bend—the Cape Riviera—some of the most stunning landscape in Africa, more spectacular than the South of France, he turns serious.

"One of those guys killed was my ex-lover. Sergio de Castro. Great guy."

"Oh, I'm sorry," I say, recalling that name.

"It's okay. I have a boyfriend now. But I'm going to the funeral in two days to show my respects."

I feel this would be disturbing for me to attend, but I also feel as though something's been murdered in me too. Hope perhaps?

Along Camps Bay Road we pass Kloofnek Road, leading to Table Mountain. As we watch Ahmed scuttle across the road I hop into the front seat. The driver leans over and says conspiratorially, "Be careful. Black people can be dangerous."

I say, "Do you really think so?"

In Pretoria I noted that thieving desperation is high. My friend had a break-in every month. Persistent thieves got through barred windows for as little as a couple of kitchen pots and pans. Culprits are usually poor and black. In Green Point, Cape Town, as I am walking, looking for a restaurant, a black guy approaches me to sell cocaine, but he looks as though he could just as easily hustle his way into my bed. Crime does not consist only of young black men in South Africa; many white guys help bolster the statistics. All involved in the Sizzlers murders are white. It's just that economic realities of abject poverty are harsh.

"It's funny," the driver continues. "What the U.S. is doing to Al Qaeda now is what our government was doing to the African National Congress a few years ago. They were treated as terrorists." Not being sure that the parallel is quite sound, I nod blandly, "Yes, perhaps that's true." Rian Malan is my guide into the hard hearts of White South Africa. Showing interest in black people is tolerated only in foreigners, he claims. For white Afrikaners this is an absolute no-no, and you will be instantly labeled a traitor. They can persuade themselves it's due to our naivete, our ignorance of what really goes on. But in this driver I note a new kind of balance, being able to see where formerly they were unjust. I notice the driver's uncommonly glacial gray eyes, as I thank him and say good-bye.

### *"Please don't overreact. Don't do anything stupid."*

Table Mountain is the perfect backdrop for some grand end-it-all finale. An eagle can descend from on high and plummet down gracefully, but humans can't; they have to use the cable car. For those with a death wish, Table Mountain is perhaps not the most advisable place to spend a hot afternoon. Death from here might be beautifully strange, but that's not for me to decide. A body found on the rocks would hardly make a dent in the current headlines anyhow with the furor over the gay murders. The mountain's grand sweeping precipices plunge downward on either side, devastatingly abrupt. It's flanked by oceans: facing south, to the left is the Indian Ocean and False Bay, to the right, the Atlantic from whence this great slab of rock emerged; if you allow your eye to run straight ahead, there's the Antarctic, and far over the curved horizon line, the South Pole. Several scraggy peaks of varying size and shape jut into the air from different angles down to the rocky treacherous coastline. These are the Twelve Apostles, and you can well imagine them hooded and cloaked, bent in resignation to the vicious elements. This after all is the Cape Horn, famous for its howling winds and calamitous tides.

I am sitting 3,500 feet high, on clods of earth that have more variety of plant species than the whole of the British Isles, and, as I gaze at these great distances I feel less joy and wonder than I do dismay at my past errors my incurable wanderlust, welling up from tectonic rock fissures. This feeling suppurates with the dull certainty of lava. This is the farthest point I've reached. All roads, the train journey, the affair are stumped at this: the only way for me to go now is back. Back down to the cable car that hangs over the city. Back home to more of the same-old stuff. Feeling this down is the ultimate luxury, since I have paid to come here. I didn't factor into my holiday a life-altering depression. That was extra. It is more comforting to be miserable in more familiar surroundings instead of paying to be a sad, white blotch on an alien landscape.

The British couple who run my guest house are not fazed by the murders. This is not saying that people are unflappable here. *Pragmatic* might be a better word. Cape Town is genuinely beautiful, and it's not expensive. The guest house owners potter on with their garden azaleas, or prepare scrambled eggs, fry bacon, do the chores, make shopping lists, remaining apparently cheerful, contented and, most important, busy. Everything tip-top and double locked, battened down with bars on the windows, double security locks. Upstairs in my attic room a wicked wind beats on the glass in the window frame, making it shudder. Then it screeches on up the mountainside toward the great monolith of rock towering behind.

Travel brochures proclaim Cape Town as a new gay paradise. That's what travel brochures are supposed to do, fly toy flags to attract foreign cash. For "paradise" just read natural beauty, which gay people may inhabit like anyone else. Like most things, the picture is often better than the reality. Cape Town is also a very religious city, and some local citizens, especially Muslims, are not happy with this pink tag. The Cape Town scene, centered around Green Point and Waterkrant Street, is nice enough, not overly prominent, though it is organized and well run. It has a few bars and restaurants that are much freer and less threatening than Jo'burg's. You don't hang around at a loose end in central Jo'burg in the early hours of the morning after you've spilled out of the clubs. You arrange for someone to come by car to collect you. Cape Town is more relaxed, and friendlier. Saunas however tend to be peopled with the older, larger sort of men who can afford to take up space in a Jacuzzi and procure young hustlers. This is the business of pleasure: tightly controlled, centered around drinking, eating, carousing, cruising, and sex. Though Cape Town has a pride march to its credit, and the MCQP (Mother City Queer Project), a mega costume party, once a city gets to this level of openness and sophistication, it begins to lose local distinction and assumes the mantel of *anytown-anywhere's* scene. It's as though wherever a gay scene manifests, it becomes a great leveler.

I'm ordering a vodka and Coke when I get this magnificent smile from across the disco bar. This is Reginald, or Reggie. He has no job and no money, and he likes foreigners because they buy him drinks so he can enjoy himself. He's cute and unaccountably happy. Compared to me, that's not hard. Perhaps it will be infectious, I think. Tall and slender, with a coffee-cream skin, and very agile on the dance floor, he's from the mixed colored outer township sprawl. He gets by somehow. He says he wants to work in the tourist industry.

"Just so you can get laid?" I ask, teasing.

"Yes," He says, grinning. "Why not?"

"Let's get to 'work' then," I say.

Reggie's mouth drops. Then the magnificent smile breaks over his face. He laughs from his shoulders. "You are so funny. You couldn't buy me a drink, could you? You can be my baby tonight."

So I'm someone's baby again—that fast. The word sours in my mouth.

Next day, I need to take to the sea. Nelson Mandela spent twenty-seven years in a tiny prison cell on Robben Island. This famous experience has all the makings of a legend, but the isolation must have been insufferable. He got through it by educating himself. This island is now a nature reserve housing rare species of birds. During World War II it was used as a military base against the German submarine attacks. The box cell Mandela inhabited is no bigger than a bathroom stripped of decoration, something Van Gogh might paint in explosive yellows and grays. Here Mandela planned how he would carve out his place in history. That it is now a museum, generating tourist income, is a tribute to the power of a contemplative mind, to an innate resilience and tenacity. The guide is an ex-convict himself, now pot-bellied, almost blind. He tells of routine torture and deprivation. Robben Island is a remote outcrop, cut off at the tip of the continent. The idea of swimming to shore in these treacherous waters would cause the best athletes to quake.

Back on the ferry, people are pointing to the famous "tablecloth." This is a layer of mist that sits on the top of the luminous mountain. It prevents anyone using the cable car because there'd be nothing to see—your head would literally be in the clouds. This layer of low cloud spreads on the flat-topped mountain and clings to its edges, just like carefully arranged drapery in a painting. The ferry back to the Victoria and Albert Waterfront juts across the waves, slamming hard into the curved tips. The exhilarating spray hits everyone full on till hiding from it becomes useless and we stand, plain soaking wet.

Later that evening, with Reggie licking my ear, I'm standing on Bree Street in the gay district, eavesdropping a cabaret voice drawling out in the street. It's a drag queen saying to her captive audience, "Have you noticed how women's problems are caused by Men? Like MENstruation, MENopause, MENtal illness. . . ." The Drag Queen waits for the laughs to kick in. Then, at the right moment, chirps,

"Women get their own back with HERnias, HERpes, hemHER-rhoids."

*Yeah,* I think to myself. *Have you heard the joke about the online date that goes tragically wrong? No? Well, it's a classic: This guy travels thousands of miles to meet a potential lover. One guy ends up in tears; the other has a breakdown and goes into therapy.* Hilarious? No. Just a symptom of a wider problem of longing for otherness. Only those who suffer it will know how it feels. Of never belonging anywhere but where your heart leads. I had come to him in good faith and was overawed with my chosen Tswana lover at the Jo'burg airport. He was wearing a tight-fitting red shirt with African designs on it. He looked simple and beautiful, quiet and intense. He'd brought his cousin to drive us to Pretoria. He was gentle and considerate of me and my welfare, and for the first few days I was in a honeymoon swirl. We made love on his bed every night. I took him as he wished. When his friend, the one who'd done something bad to him that I was forbidden to mention, dropped us off one night from drinks downtown and turned to us and asked, "So what are you guys going to do now?"

"We're going to make wild passionate love," said my lover, who I then hoped would always say such things. I felt vindicated, that this was really what *he* wanted. It wasn't just *my* imagination. Sure enough, I felt that he was returning the passion that surged within me as we writhed on the bed and held each other. I did not suspect a trap. Though I did begin to think I was also somewhat of an intruder into his intricate web of personal anguish, he certainly seemed to love me back, and it was unnerving to see him become increasingly distant, like he had too many things he didn't want to tell me, and as though I would just blunder through them making everything worse. I had no idea he was having sudden reservations. I believed all the beautiful words in our e-mail correspondence, that he was looking for a true love, someone for whom he would cross continents, someone just like me. He kissed me deeply. He did not seem to reject my caresses. I was his lover from London and he was my new Tswana boy.

After all, I had come all this way just for him, even knowing his HIV status. This was either heroic or plain foolish. Most hard-bitten folk would opt for the latter explanation. But the act humbled him, he claimed, such a blind date, across continents, age, race, and income brackets. I took a great risk, as did he for welcoming me into his home. Yet it didn't stop him, after a week, from saying those words that still have the power to jar my nerves, that he did not feel what I felt. This person was more of a stranger on leaving than he was before we met. More isolated. He was deeply troubled. I suspected also that he had just thought he wanted me, but when he got me, he didn't want it, the situation, validating the adage of being careful what you wish for. He had a mesh of problems I could scarcely imagine, not least of which now was guilt for encouraging me to come, and for being so excited that it was all happening. It was only later that I began to see that maybe he'd released me from a terrible bind, a well of love and poison, and that to be sucked into his sweet, bitter life would curtail all of what made mine desirable. To have pretended then to love would have been worse. Perhaps he was cutting me free?

Those disillusioned by love and life scoff and point always to neediness and desperation as no-win factors to establish a relationship. It hadn't a hope in hell of working out, especially in South Africa. Or had it? Wouldn't it have been better to stay at home? The worst is when I see a handsome black and white gay couple stroll idly along Cape Town's Main Road. They're wearing disco shirts and they are obviously happy, obviously staying together in the same hotel room. Why is this so hard to watch? It's the love story I wrote for myself that didn't happen, with these unknown actors in roles cut out for me and him.

### "Let's just be friends."

There's tourism for sex, tourism for love, and tourism for tourism's sake. I don't know which is the sadder variety. Sex tourism may be unseemly and exploitative, but at least it's a practical exchange. It does not aspire to be what it is not. Love tourism is all tilting at windmills, high in costly illusions. The danger is you bring ruins to ruins. Yet, even the best, most intelligent people can succumb to the addiction of falling in love on the net, which, strangely in this wham-bam world, allows for all old-fashioned courtship rituals to flourish, the

kind we cannot find in bars or clubs. This intimacy crystallizes an image of the lover much closer to our fugitive ideal. That is surely worth
traveling across cultures to find? Sticking within the tribe has not
proved that much better as I witness countless relationships of friends
start and break up. Yet, the reality of the "other" can be a cold water
bath. This doesn't mean it's always in vain. The yearning for that ideal
lover abroad may be equated to the degree of dislike for your home
town, but it can, and does, happen. We just need to take more stock
of what we lack in our back yard that we have to pose others elsewhere
as love saviors.

Perhaps we are positioned in locations to expand or contract, as the
imperatives of personal growth dictate. The more painful it is, the
deeper the disorder that must be resolved. If it triggers the first genuine need for professional help, then maybe it's of some use. After years
of pooh-poohing the value of psychotherapists, the breed of counselor
I had always deemed parasites, I felt a seismic change. Advice given to
me as a child was of the old-school, just-pull-yourself-together variety. That no longer worked. In South Africa, for the first time, I
needed help to know where I was going with all this coming and
going.

## "My best friend raped me, but don't say anything about it please."

South Africa reminds me now of a multiplex wound, one that fes-
ters no matter what kind of treatment is applied, no matter how
many fingers, clean or dirty, are poked into it, no matter how much
money is poured in. This country's soil smells queer, is soaked in
blood, as C. G. Jung said upon arriving in Africa. This curious odor
rises to boiling point in thunderstorms across Gauteng province.
Tragic events are the norm. Yet, it's redeemable. Like any other country, there has to be something better for it, in spite of everything. We
fondly imagine that out of tragedy comes some new-formed beast
more able to face the truths that people have long denied. People are
in need of love here, same as anywhere. They must look only to them-

selves. My wish to collapse the traditional black equals evil, white equals virtue metaphors is unlikely to be granted. History and hardheads with a lifetime invested in hatred and revenge will see that old feuds are well stoked. Everyone comes with a race or price tag, especially in South Africa, with AIDS and rape statistics so high that it makes you fear the worst, makes you fear that the problem is so humungous that it's without solution. Now I see that when you have nothing else, sometimes a grudge, a sense of lingering injustice, is the only thing you've got to keep you going. The bitterness of your hope gives you juice to drink.

### *"I believe relationships can only work through communication. As long as you talk, it's okay"*

I fly back to Jo'burg, unprepared to repeat the long train journey back across Mordor country. I've done my dues here. I'm not sure if I will ever return. I phone and text but no answers come. It's as though someone who once signified large has now rendered himself invisible behind the veil of "stranger." There are some things I left behind in Pretoria, a Dirk Bikkembergs belt, a navy blue shirt. I plead with him to send me these things, to at least talk, or even come to see me off, but he becomes adept at eluding me, enmeshed in a complex world of his own problems and anxieties, medications, the cost of living, loan debts, robberies, the guilt of having lured someone so far only to draw a blank check of feelings. His silence tells me of his confusion.

Back home, I ask him to send me at least the belt, which was a valued present. He promises and promises, saying he never meant to hurt or harm. The belt never comes. It will most likely hang in his cupboard, untouched, till perhaps snatched by a burglar. Now, watching extraordinary films like *Something of Value* with Rock Hudson and Sidney Poitier, about men, one white, one black, who bonded across tribal lines with, and who talk of somehow being married to the rugged beauty of Africa, I begin to know what they mean.

# ✋ 11      The Broken Promise

*Dayton Estes*

It has been almost fifty years since I reneged on a promise I made to Claudio who more than adequately fulfilled his end of the bargain to put at my disposal a handsome eighteen-year-old German boy for as long and as often as I wanted. Even worse, I treated the whole matter as a joke and ended up paying dearly for my bad judgment and American naivete.

I had received a Fulbright scholarship to study Germanics at the Karl-Eberhard Universität in Tübingen, a quaint university town in southwest Germany. Like all new students, I was very lonely at the beginning of the semester and sought out other students for companionship. A small, tightly knit group of Germans, made of five guys and two girls, Brigitte and Eva, eventually befriended me. We met daily in the late afternoon in a small pub named Tante Emilie's, owned by an old lady who had saved many in the town from starvation during the war years. Old Emilie was a legend already for this, and was rumored to have also been Enrico Caruso's mistress in happier times.

Although Eva was engaged to Dieter, one of the boys in the group, Brigitte had been and remained her first love all through high school. Brigitte, however, was dating Wolfgang, another member of the group. Being unaware of these entanglements I followed my macho American instincts, brashly shoved Wolfgang aside, and made a play for Brigitte. I guess I was also desperately hoping once and for all to dispel the fear that I was homosexual. It didn't work, of course, and I finally realized that I could no longer fake being straight and drag a wife and eventually children through the rest of my life. Of course, "coming out" was not a rational option at that time in the late 1950s, even in Germany, and my play for Brigitte was likewise considered a divisive act in the group. I was, however, finally honest with Brigitte about my sexuality, which only exacerbated in her a sense of rejection. Eva stood by to encourage the incipient rancor and plotted, I was later to find out, to get rid of me. I was an American, after all, and World War II had ended only thirteen years before. Many upper-class Germans still had reservations (read *prejudices*) against us. Nonetheless, we still hung together, drank beer in the late afternoon, and continued to discuss world problems for the rest of the fall semester.

One afternoon in early February, when the new semester had begun, I was having my dinner before going to class when suddenly a well-dressed man, a couple of years older than I, perhaps about thirty, appeared at my table. He asked if he might join me, and before I could answer he had seated himself, apologizing for being so forward. I assumed that he was another one of the former students the old lady counted among her loyal clientele. The gentleman appeared rather finicky but not unpleasant, though not a person I would normally take to. However, I was immediately put on my guard, when he introduced himself, "My name, Herr Estes, is Claudio, Claudio Oettinger. You are *Amerikaner*, yes?" It was not hard to know that I was an American, but he also knew my name. His family, he claimed, owned the Gasthof am Schloß, a small inn directly across from Hohentübingen, the town's sixteenth century castle, adding, "I am manager of the restaurant." Though you really couldn't tell about Germans because the social mannerisms were different, somehow I surmised he was a homosexual. He was polite and a good conversationalist; however, it didn't take long for him to get down to business.

Since it was the beginning of the spring semester, the Burschenschaften, or social fraternities, were paying their traditional visit to all the bars, and Tante Emilie's had apparently been scheduled for that day. It was like a scene from *The Student Prince,* except this was real, the scars on the boys' cheeks were genuine, and most "brothers" were tall, blond, looked affluent, and were quite drunk. Claudio began to comment pointedly on several of the more Nordic types here and there among the boisterous group, mentioning that it was his pleasure to be acquainted personally with some individuals among the *gentlemen students,* adding proudly that at times two or three of them would accord him the honor of visiting his father's pub and staying overnight in the inn upstairs. He would probably have divulged more information about some of the better looking among the boys, but just then he happened to spot among my books *The Journals of André Gide.* He was also familiar with *Corydon* as well as the *Immoralist.* When I asked him if he had read the latter two works, he confessed that he had indeed read them, but in German translation. He continued that he wasn't so fortunate as to be a scholar, but rather a businessman who would be privileged, perhaps in the near future, to manage and eventually to inherit the Gasthof am Schloß, as had his father and his father's father and so forth for generations back at least to the late 1600s. Furthermore, he would shortly also be encouraged into a marriage of convenience, "How you say—an *inconvenience* for me, though," and he smiled demurely at his own pun. Yet he was willing to enter a marriage, because once he had sired an heir, he could more or less take advantage of the double standard, "Which we in Europe know so well and enjoy so gladly."

"Have you perhaps a little treasure in America? How you say it— a little girl?"

"No, not yet, I guess I'm just not so lucky."

"Perhaps a beautiful boy is your best friend, I think."

I shifted positions, "Uh, no."

"*Schade!* Too bad, as you say. You see, I am acquainted with Fräulein Eva Roth. I believe you know her, I have seen you with her and friends, particularly one girlfriend, Fräulein Brigitte Wei... *Nein* ... Weis ... *Ach,* I cannot remember her last name."

"You mean, Brigitte Weizsäcker?" and I began to fold up the newspaper I was reading and fumbled around in my book sack, packing my books to leave.

"No matter! She is of no concern to me. The purpose of my visit to you here in this *place,* is that I have had occasion to observe you, and you are very attractive and virile, and, besides, I believe you were also a soldier in the American army, yes? The American soldiers, please pardon me, look so strong and muscular in their sexy underwear. Would you join me one evening for dinner? I think you will find the evening, the dinner, and wine to your liking, and afterward, if you are willing and agree to stay the night, I will make my pleasure well worth your while. In addition, I know a delightful boy whom I will send to you to be your friend as often as you wish and for the rest of the time you are in Tübingen. I would like also to get to know you very well."

We were both finished, he with his beer, I with my goulash and black bread. I had to go to class in fifteen minutes.

"Allow me, the repast is—how you say?—my pleasure. Please excuse me if I embarrass you, I did not mean to, only to be of help. You see, Europe is older and otherwise from America, and one may deal in Europe with matters of a delicate nature very discreetly, but at the same time very differently, perhaps, from in America. But I stray. As for the boy, I will send him to you soon as a token of my expectation, as well as my appreciation. I know where you live, but it is better that he first meet you here some evening or perhaps at some other pub, and then you may take him to your bed, or as you wish."

At first, I thought the guy was nuts or at least way out in left field, but he had my number all right. No doubt where and from whom he had got his information about me, and there was no use denying, so I jokingly agreed to his offer, addressing him with the familiar *du,* "Okay, Claudio, a deal then!" We shook hands as we parted company, and I thought that would be the end of the matter. Where I come from nobody makes a deal with a queer or prostitutes himself to a fairy, I thought, and it didn't matter that I was of that ilk, "You just didn't deal with people like that on the up and up, they don't count anyway." But who the hell cares? I thought. At the invitation of the Fulbright Commission I was going to Berlin along with the five other Fulbright students in Tübingen, and I didn't have to worry about this dump of a town. I would get out for a while, return after two weeks and then read, as they say, the "fine print." Surely by that time the whole matter would have blown over.

It was about a week after I had come back from Berlin, the middle of March and the spring semester was well underway. The fraternities, however, were still involved in making their bedraggled rounds in bar after bar, singing all the old German folk and drinking songs, fulfilling a centuries old ritual, standing up at times, *prosting* Aunt Emilie, then one another as well as the other clientele, sitting down and getting drunk, again rising, *prosting* . . . it didn't stop. Suddenly a stream of water gushed under the table. A drunk brother could just not make it outside to the toilet or else didn't try. Nobody paid the least attention, except for a dog which unfortunately was lying in what became an intermittent stream. When the dog stood up and shook himself, his master and all the surrounding drinkers got wet, but they were too juiced up to really care. After the good tante closed at one a.m., most would end up across the street at the Neckar Mühlerei and continue their bacchanalia in that bar until four a.m. Fortunately attendance in German lectures is not enforced or even checked.

After I had moved across the street with the boisterous crowd, I noticed a good-looking boy had joined the drinkers at a long table. He was swarthy, his dark brown hair neatly groomed and combed. His hands looked thin and strong, but not the artistic hands of a pianist, not soft like those of a student, nor callous like those of an athlete who might take part in the many regattas in Tübingen. He sang with gusto the old nationalistic folk songs, but he drank sparingly and remained sober. I kept staring at him in such a way that would have been inexcusable in the United States. He was beautiful but masculine, small and muscular. He had the whitest teeth, and I noticed he didn't smoke. That was odd for a German student and particularly for a German teenager. Even in my drunken stupor that night, I remember thinking, *Could that be the boy Claudio . . . no, not that boy, surely.*

About a week later, it had turned cold and the wind was blowing gale force around the buildings and through the middle of town when I caught sight of Claudio, and he saw me simultaneously. "Hallo," he called and came running up breathless, "He pleases you?" and then, "You like him?"

"Who?"

"Why, Hansjörg! The boy who sat at your table at the Neckar Mühlerei a week ago last Tuesday? You like him, yes? Now will you grant me the honor and privilege of entertaining you one evening and accept my invitation for the night? That is all I ask in return and please wear that military underwear."

"Sure, Claudio, sure! Talk to you later!" I naively continued to think he was joking. What would he want with me, twenty-seven years old, when he could have that kid? Anyhow Claudio was so bourgeois, I thought, a cheap imitation of Gustav Aschenbach in Thomas Mann's *Death in Venice.* I suddenly realized I had begun to take on the prejudices of the German intelligentsia. Still, I frankly need have nothing more to do with him, and any so-called "promise" I supposedly made to him regarding sexual matters, especially aberrant sex, was ludicrous, even if a handsome boy was involved. And yet, the German idea, no matter how vague, of the inviolability of an oral contract continued to haunt me.

It was the sixth of April. Although not warm by the southern American standards of my upbringing, there was still the sense spring was in the air. That evening, I went to Tante Emilie, grabbed a beer from a crate outside the door, entered, greeted everyone, and sat down. It was a small bar, really just a room and served only beer which was customarily stashed outside in a storage room that was unlocked during business hours. A hot plate and a small refrigerator served to cook soup and to store perishables, and except for the tables and benches that was all there was.

The door opened and the kid entered. He greeted all the customers, as is the custom in Germany, though he basically knew no one except Mammele, the new owner who had taken over after Aunt Emilie's death while I was in Berlin. Hansjörg came over to my table, greeted me, shook my hand, and asked if he might join me. "Please do!"

My God, was he good-looking, even more so up close than he had been that night across the street in the Neckar Mühlerei. He addressed me with the familiar *du* as soon as we began to talk. I found out he had just celebrated his eighteenth birthday and that he and the remainder of his family were refugees from East Germany, but they had been living in Tübingen for a little over five years. He was now apprenticed to a dental technician and would have completed his apprenticeship in three years.

He had been a student, but had decided he needed to make whatever money he could to help out his family who had originally lived in Breslau, now, by treaty, Wroclaw, Poland. He had been lucky even to be alive after the invading Soviet troops had discovered him and his family cowering in a cellar. The soldiers, although ignoring the two children, had bayonetted his father on the spot and raped his mother who was now employed as a maid, trying to make a home in West Germany. They had been quite well-off before the war. He vaguely remembered being in Breslau the latter days of the war, before the local Jews were loaded on cattle cars and transported to Auschwitz.

"Why don't we get out of all this smoke?" he suggested. He had already begun to cough from the cigarette and pipe smoke billowing up over every table. I stuffed a couple of bottles of beer in my coat pockets; Hansjörg carried his, for he had no coat. Outside we passed by students downing the local brew and lolling around in the early spring warmth on the *Neckarmauer,* a centuries-old stone wall that ran alongside the Neckar River, which flowed through town. Now and then we paused to watch as students pole-rafted on the quiet waters of the Neckar, each raft lit by a Japanese lantern. We then trudged up the steep cobblestone street to the castle, our arms around each other, singing the drinking songs we had not joined in on at the bar, so intent were we in talking. My fingers had already crept into his shirt, sought out, found and were rubbing his small nipples, now hard. We crossed over the bridge spanning the moat of the castle and entered its great cobblestone courtyard. The castle had been converted into a clinic. Hansjörg seemed to know his way around and told me that he had once worked in one of the offices here. We were planning to climb up to the castle's highest wall and watch the flickering lights of Tübingen and the gray outline of the Swabian Alb, a mountain range to the south. High above the town, however, the winds showed no mercy, and the warm congenial night quickly turned into an icy shudder. I felt Hansjörg's body shiver in the cold and I took off my coat and covered us both as best I could. We soon climbed down and crouched in a corner near the base out of the wind. My hand continued to move quickly around inside his shirt ostensibly trying to rub him to keep him warm, but now and again touching his left nipple, which was still hard. My fingers delicately played around in the sparse hairs of his armpit, and then my hand, which seemed to have a mind of its own, would mischievously run up and down the lean ribs. Not an ounce of fat.

Suddenly, he turned to me and kissed me on the cheek and then nestled his head under my neck, remaining there for just a few seconds before undoing his belt and unzipping his pants. I took his already erect penis in my hand, he was huge, and gently pulled back the foreskin. "*Magst du mich auch?*" he asked. "Do you also like me?"

"*Ja,* very much," I said, as I bent down, surrendering my coat to his shivering body, and took him into my mouth. I was relatively new to all this, but I instinctively knew what to do the first time I ever did it, and I knew how to do it, and I knew I liked what I was doing. It didn't take long before he groaned and again his body trembled. At first I didn't know if it was from the sudden icy blast or from orgasm. And then, temporarily gagging, I said, "Let's go. Either you won't have a coat, or else I won't have a coat."

"But you, you, I want you, too," he protested.

"Too cold. We can postpone it. Let's get out of here." And we left the empty bottles stacked neatly in a trash can and went down to the entrance, the way we had come in. The bridge over the moat was the only way out, but the monstrous oak gate had been locked and bolted and the moat was much too steep and deep to navigate.

"I forgot to tell you, well, I really just forgot. The gate is locked every night at ten o'clock."

"Well, it wasn't locked at least one night at ten," I quipped. "How're we going to get out of here? We can't stay here and freeze to death, and I don't want to break into any of the buildings. Do you know any other way out?"

"Look, there is one way, but it may be blocked."

"Let's try it anyway."

"Good, but it is also dangerous."

"Anything is better than dying of cold here or being mistaken for burglars by the police."

Once again we trudged up to the highest level of the mountain within the castle precincts, this time, though, not going to the high wall but over behind the highest buildings on the northern side. We slowly picked our way alongside the wall until Hansjörg found a small opening just large enough to crawl through. It took both of us to creak open the rusty iron barrier. This all-but-hidden exit had been intended as an escape hatch for the nobility in case the castle was under siege and fell to a marauding army. We then clambered down a steep slope on the side of the mountain which had been fortified like a battlefield in World War I, replete with barbed wire strands, still discouraging even modern-day trespassers.

"First, I go, and then you, yes?" We slid down the gravel, trying to grab hold of each post supporting the wire, sometimes missing, skinning our arms or rear ends on the rocks and coarse dirt, sometimes scratching an arm or a leg on the barbed wire. Finally, we landed on the top of a stone or brick wall that must have been at least twenty-five or thirty feet high, maybe higher. I couldn't survey the layout beneath us in the dim light of the moon, otherwise I would have panicked from the sheer height of the wall. No way to jump down that wall without breaking every bone in our bodies, when suddenly again Hansjörg had an idea. A weekend cottage was located somewhere in the vicinity and abutted the wall. If we could find that house, he thought, a ladder or a pole might just be leaning against the wall and we could climb down. We finally spotted the house, but no pole or ladder made our lives so lucky. Thank God for the moon, not full, but enough to see vague outlines of things.

"Look, *ein Scheißhaufen!*" he whispered, because a light shone out a window, and he meant literally "a pile of shit," cow manure, horse manure, maybe even human from pumping out outdoor toilets. "I'll jump on the top of the house and then roll off onto the pile, get down and make a run for the barbed wire fence surrounding the house, then climb up on it or through it and out. Are you with me?"

I didn't have to make up my mind or have time to answer. The icy wind did that for me, and the beer that I had been drinking all evening made it easier not to resist my instinct to run and probably kept me from tensing up and breaking any bones on the terra-cotta roof of the weekend house. My olfactory senses were likewise numb when I rolled into the cow or horse manure—at least it turned out not to be human—and then the wind and beer again made me fight my way desperately up and through the barbed wire fence that protected one

of Tübingen's distinguished lawyers or professors or well-heeled business men and his mistress from the prying eyes of a bourgeois and
moralistic society, perhaps even from a wife insanely and justifiably
jealous. Though a barbed wire fence might keep burglars out, it
couldn't keep us in.

An angry voice threw open the door. "Who's there? Who's there?
Quick! Call the police! Help! Help!"

He or she did indeed call the police while the old man stood at the
door screaming. Hansjörg and I had not quite got to the bottom of
the wooded mountain before we heard the beep of a police cruiser and
saw in the distance a blue light. We managed to make it back to my
place undetected. I didn't invite him in because I was renting a room
from the assistant chief of police, Herr Hirzel, which was advanta-
geous in many ways, just not tonight. We caught sight of him coming
down the steps to report for emergency duty at the police station two
blocks away. I hurried up the stairs, and Hansjörg hurried home,
though I never did find out where *home* was.

Nothing ever came of the castle episode because Herr Hirzel and
the rest of the constables couldn't figure why burglars would break in,
yet steal nothing. A blurb in the *Schwäbisches Tagblatt,* the local newspaper, later on in the week surmised that punks had broken into the
courtyard of the castle but had been scared away by policemen and
stolen nothing. No mention was made of how they might have gotten
away. I had lost my glasses somewhere in the process, maybe on that
pile of cow or horse manure, but I wasn't about to go to lost and found
at the police station to report the American-made glasses missing.

The next evening about dinnertime Hansjörg stopped by my room
to see me. We played around a little, and he took care of the unfin-
ished business from the castle. At that time I had just purchased two
LP records of Bach's Brandenburg concertos, and I lent them to him
because he claimed also to like Baroque music. I was very proud of the
LP records, which were terribly expensive on the German market. I
had no record player at the time and was planning to take the recordings, a collector's item, back to the United States. He promised to
take good care of them. I really enjoyed having Hansjörg around.
Hansjörg—Hänsle as I had begun to call him affectionately—wasn't

the sharpest tool in the shed, but I liked him a lot, and he and I saw each other often for the next month until one day, he all of a sudden said, "I think you should go visit Claudio."

"Claudio? Why? He's just an old maid. He bores me."

"*Nein*! He is my friend. I like him, and I think you should visit him. I go now." And that was the last time Hansjörg came to my room and, in effect, the last time I was with him. I didn't know where he lived so I couldn't call or go find him, and visiting Claudio continued to be a bad scene in my estimation. After that I saw Hanjörg only twice: once was from a distance just as his bus was pulling off from the curb, and once I almost ran into him, called and tried to follow him, but he ducked into a building and disappeared.

Other things changed, too. I found my tight-knit group of friends no longer tight-knit, in fact, not really friends. They no longer frequented Tante Emilie's, and now whenever I showed up I realized that I was not greeted by the other students. They were, of course, polite, but never friendly as they had been. Sometimes I thought or imagined I heard a snicker when I entered the bar, or saw students staring at me and laughing among themselves, and, it seemed to me, nodding in my direction. Nevertheless, the feeling could have been brought on by the fact I stood out as an American, or perhaps it was that "instinct for survival," at times erroneously or superficially dismissed as "homosexual paranoia." I know well the discomfort; I still feel it sometimes even after fifty years. Still worse, Brigitte kept sending word to me that she had cancer of the uterus and wanted me to come to Stuttgart to visit her, for she had dropped out of school. But I figured she had just had an abortion.

An unpleasant month passed and Hänsle didn't return the LPs. Moreover, the end of the semester had already come. I was leaving Tübingen the next week for Hamburg and then New York. I had my hands full in packing and getting my papers in order. To be sure, I wanted my LPs back, but, the truth of the matter is that I very much wanted to see Hansjörg once again before I left.

One day before my departure I encountered Claudio in town as he was leaving the city hall. No way to avoid him, so I said hello, shook

hands, and told him I wanted to say *Auf Wiedersehen*. I couldn't think
of anything else to say.

"Have you perhaps forgotten something else?" he asked, his eyes
not hostile, yet not friendly.

"Uh, no, I don't think so. Oh, yes, one thing—if you see Hansjörg,
please remind him he promised to return my recordings of the
Brandenburg concertos." Claudio turned and walked on.

Early the next morning Frau Hirzel, my landlady, said her good-
byes, but Herr Hirzel was on duty at the police station. I went to take
one last look at the center of town, and then went to the bank to close
my checking account. The train left that afternoon at 15:16, and my
baggage was already at the station. I returned to my room to check
one last time for anything I might have forgotten, but really it was really just to take one last look. Leaning against the front door of the
apartment was one of my two LPs. When I pulled the record out of
the jacket to check it, it looked as if somebody had taken a nail or a
knife, or maybe a pair of scissors and made deep scratches in the vinyl.
Scribbled in pen on the record jacket, *"Schade um die Platte!"* it said.
"Sorry about the record!"

I saw Claudio one more time eighteen years later. I had gone to
Germany to spend a month with friends in the Palatinate, in the
south of the country. On my way from there to Italy I detoured
through Tübingen for old time's sake. The town hadn't changed
much. The house in which I had rented a room from Herr and Frau
Hirzel was still there, and I was tempted to post a paper sign on the
right side of the door "officially" designating it the *Esteshaus,* thus following the German tradition of naming a house or building after a famous person who has lived or worked there, but I thought better of it!

A convention was being held in town, and rooms were scarce. So, as
luck would have it, I had to spend the night in the Gasthof am Schloß.
In the morning as I was checking out I caught sight of someone who
looked like he might just be Claudio, eighteen years older. He was
dressed in a white shirt, black bow tie, and black trousers, and was
puttering around in the dining room, setting up for lunch, and looking quite officious.

If that was Claudio, well, I guess he had inherited the business.

# The Ukimwi Road

*Richard Burnett*

We left cold Nairobi in July and drove deep into the Great Rift Valley south towards Tanzania. I was with Seb, my dearest friend with whom I had backpacked much of the world. Our African odyssey had begun months earlier on the Mediterranean coast as we drove south from Cairo. Once in sub-Saharan Africa, we witnessed the great migrations north throughout the Rift Valley. The big cats followed the herds of millions of wildebeests from the golden Serengeti plains to the Masai Mara. I felt a sense of euphoric homecoming as Seb and I pushed farther and farther southeast to the coast where we would make new friends and see my family again.

Our Bedford was a brand-new old truck that had been put together only the night before, refitted with four-wheel drive. In Africa even brand-new parts are secondhand. There were a dozen passengers, along with Seb and myself, our guide Kathy, and a crew of three Tanzanians. My favorite was our cook Justin. He was not as tall as I was, but he was lanky and strong all over, with beautiful arms, lips, and high cheekbones. We'd gone shopping at the food market together in Nairobi. I caught my breath several times watching him bargain in the market. He gestured with his hands, commanding much respect. When he turned to smile at me I wanted those hands on me. We loaded the thirty-year-old Bedford with bread, fruits, and vegetables, a couple of crates of beer, cheap meat, and Spam, then strapped, snapped, and tied on our canvas roof and side panels.

We had to get to Tanzania before dusk, and drove 200 kilometers through Amboseli to the border town of Namanga in about eight hours. Justin did not have a Tanzanian passport, but he had the spe-

*Looking for Love in Faraway Places*
© 2007 The Haworth Press, Inc. All rights reserved.
doi:10.1300/5366_12

cial work visa that allows Kenyans, Ugandans, and Tanzanians to work in one another's countries. I also learned upon leaving Nairobi that Canadians needed a visa to enter Tanzania—retribution for a Canadian diplomat's rebuke of a Tanzanian policy two days earlier.

I had dual British and Canadian citizenship because my parents had fled civil unrest in Colonial Africa and gave birth to me in Canada. The Kenyan customs officers at Namanga refused to give me an exit stamp on my British passport since I had entered with my Canadian passport. Twenty minutes after that debacle I found myself in Justin's home country without the required visa. I slipped ten American dollars inside my Canadian passport and gave it to a proud woman, dressed in navy blue, looming above me.

She opened it. "What's this?" she asked, holding up the American bill clearly for all to see.

"The fee to enter," I said quietly.

She stared down at me. I had finally found an honest customs officer, and instead of feeling vindicated I became quickly indignant, furious that an African official should refuse a bribe.

"A visa costs fifty dollars," the woman told me, and gave me a receipt.

I felt more shame when I turned and saw Justin watching me. I did not know what he had heard, but I could not help but feel that he just saw a disrespectful Canadian polluting his country. My face, dark from the sun, warmed as I flushed. Invisibly, I hoped, but my shame ran deeper. I was after all in the land of my forefathers, desecrating the land from where I had come.

We arrived in Arusha close to midnight and pitched our tents in the Masai Camp. Justin and his crew started a fire and began preparing our supper. It was quite cold, but thankfully there were few mosquitoes and no tsetse flies. The rest of us dragged our weary bodies to the campsite bar. It had corrugated iron walls supported by thick wooden beams, and a thatched roof. We drank up a storm around a big fire and wrote in our journals. We slowly raised our voices and our bottles as we discussed African politics. I realized I did not desire the camaraderie of young Western adults; I wanted to look up at the stars alone with Justin in a sleeping bag out in the bush.

\* \* \* \*

In a campsite atop Ngorongoro Crater one evening after dusk I helped Justin prepare supper as the cool mist settled and cloaked the mountainsides. The others were taking showers in stalls beyond our tents hidden in the mist. Justin and I filled a large iron pot with several gallons of water. We each grabbed a side and stumbled back to the fire.

"Why don't you come with us to Zimbabwe?" I asked Justin.

"I cannot. I have no passport."

Justin spoke English well enough and understood me when I spoke slowly. Swahili was his native tongue, and I understood a little of it, but didn't need to. I was just happy to sit and watch him slice open the fish for supper.

"Why doesn't the company get it for you?"

"Why don't you ask?" Justin said, but we both knew the expats in Nairobi were not going to invest in an African they believed had neither the aptitude nor the commitment to make them money. We were silent as my Bob Marley tape played on the Bedford's stereo. I watched him clean the fish and heard Seb call my name.

"Why should I go to Zimbabwe when I have what I want right here?" Justin said finally, turning his head toward me.

I stood and looked him straight in the eyes. "If you are happy here with me," I said, touching his arm, "then I am happy also."

\* \* \* \*

Justin was raised by his Masai family in a little village called USA River just east of Arusha. He was twenty-two when I met him (I was twenty-eight), and was the youngest in his family with a brother and two sisters. He did not want to raise a family in USA River and left for Dar es Salaam before his parents demanded he marry. Since the age of nineteen he'd been cooking for tourists on overland trucks in Kenya and Tanzania. The pay was minimal, but he made more than twice his wages in tips at the end of a trek. With the money he bought himself boots and baggy jeans, and he always had his toothbrush sticking out of his right-side back pocket. On this night Justin wore his Bruce Springsteen T-shirt, his favorite. When he stretched for cooking utensils in the truck the T-shirt lifted and I glimpsed his smooth lower chest. He turned to see if I was looking, and with his white teeth glimmering in a smile, he asked, "Are you hungry yet?"

After supper Justin asked me where I was from, confused by my mix of passports at the border. I told him my family was from Mauritius. I spread out a large map on the dusty soil and was happy he clearly visualized the continent; so many Africans are at a loss when given a map. I pointed out an island off the east coast of Mozambique, east of Madagascar in the Indian Ocean.

"My father is white and my mother is not," I said.

"And now you live far away," he said.

"Yes."

"Will you come back?"

The map was spread out before us, and we knelt so close to each other that I could feel his body heat. My heart was pounding, dust stuck to my sweaty palms and my throat was parched.

"Always," I whispered.

* * * *

Every morning and afternoon for the next few days we went on dusty safaris in the Serengeti, looking for big cats napping in the shade of Acacia trees, searching for leopards lounging lazily in the kopjes. One afternoon we watched a leopard stalk a herd of Thomson's gazelle for two hours, setting up a kill undetected downwind under the beating sun. While the others craned their necks watching the scene unfold through binoculars and camera zoom lenses, Justin and I sat quietly sharing a beer, our fingers touching when we both held the bottle. The leopard finally sprinted and ran down a baby gazelle. The kill was a magnificent display of skill and speed.

We left the golden plains of the Serengeti for the square, concrete storefronts of Arusha where cold showers awaited us. On the drive back we stopped in Mto Wa Mbu, a small village of artisans and craftsmen who set up shop on wooden stalls along its main street of hardened soil. The stalls have shutters held up by sticks that give shade to the Masai villagers, dressed in their red cloth, beads, and jewels. We bargained hard for stone sculptures of rhino and elephant, Masai spears and shields, earth-colored African prints and batiks. Justin tugged at my right arm and kept his hand there when he guided me to stands of fruits, vegetables, and geep—a tough chimera of goat and sheep, which was often the best meat we could purchase.

We stopped that night at the Fig Tree, a motel campsite surrounded by colorful bushes flaming red, orange, and purple. Masai tribesmen guarded the site to protect visitors from thieves and predators.

After supper, Seb and I washed our dishes and went for drinks at the Red Banana with our guide Kathy. Justin turned twenty-three that day, so we each bought him a Tusker, the local beer. The rounds grew warmer and warmer as the night wore on. At eleven o'clock the bar closed, and we all spilled onto the main street quite drunk.

It was pitch-black, no light on the streets except for our flashlights. No one was around, the stalls were closed, and all we heard were the crickets in the bush. We couldn't see the dust clouds our feet kicked up either, but we could taste them.

I bumped into Justin. "Do you know where we can relax and have another beer?" I asked, handing him my flashlight. "Let's celebrate your birthday."

He led us to a concrete building painted sky blue on the outskirts of the village. The hotel's wooden patio opened out into the bush. Just as we stepped inside, the old woman behind the bar announced last call to the few locals hanging out. We ordered Tuskers, and I took a seat directly opposite Justin as the men around us talked endlessly about soccer. We just listened and watched, but soon Justin was the center of my attention. I remembered our shoulders and legs touching, leaning against each other in the Bedford earlier in the day, and I remembered the earthy smell of his sweat. The beer was good and I was happy, and Justin had to be as well because he watched me just as intensely. We were locked onto each other so obviously, I thought, that the others must surely see what was happening.

Then Justin left the table. When he returned the men were still discussing soccer, Seb and Kathy spoke I don't know what of, and Bob Marley was pumping out of the house system.

"Oh my God! I *love* reggae!" I told Justin when he returned to the table. Bob was singing my favorite Bob song, "Is This Love." I was beaming. "That's my favorite song," I said.

Justin smiled. "I know. I made the request for you."

Soon after the song finished the bar closed and we all stumbled outside into the bush, with Justin leading us back to the Fig Tree. Seb and I had our arms entwined, but somewhere along the way I ended up walking hand in hand with Justin ahead of the others. I squeezed his hand. When he squeezed mine back I was delirious with joy.

I knew when men held hands in northern Africa it was a sign of affection and friendship, much as in the Middle East, but it was rare to see such a public display in sub-Saharan Africa. Moreover, I knew in this land that love between men, my kind of love, was kept hidden. Justin pushed away my hand and returned my flashlight as we approached the Masai guards at the Fig Tree.

He and I lingered around as Seb and Kathy said good night and crawled into their tents. I walked Justin to his motel room. He opened the door, and I turned off my flashlight and quietly stepped in behind him. My heart beat so fast as he looked at me pensively, I thought, as I stood there waiting, hoping no one else was in the room. Justin closed the door. In the blackness we found our hands and our faces and kissed.

In a deep embrace, we short stepped our way to the bed, struggling, breathing quickly, his wet lips on mine, his arms now tight around my waist. His hard and callused fingers slid up my back, and he pulled my T-shirt off above my head. I pushed him down on the bed, stripped us both of our clothes, and lay down on him, hard against each other. Our fingers and tongues lovingly caressed every cavity, eliciting quiet moans, long and exquisite, in an orgasm that left us breathless and happy.

\* \* \* \*

I rolled over at six o'clock that morning and Justin was gone. He was out making breakfast before the group and the sun awoke. I lay there quietly under the covers and watched the rising sun chase away the African cold. The room was bare, but I drank in every detail: The twisted hanger in the doorless closet, the wooden chair beneath the window, my clothes strewn about the floor. I saw only his underwear and figured he took mine. I breathed in our smells deeply, remembering, then stepped out of bed and into his underwear and my clothes. I was careful to look out the window because I didn't want the local Masai to cast out Justin. When I saw no one, I stepped outside and returned to my tent.

We drove the Bedford to Arusha that morning. Justin and the crew dropped us off at the Masai Camp en route to Nairobi. The rest of us threw our gear into another truck headed south. Justin and I exchanged addresses and a brush of the lips. We lingered a moment, then he left. I watched him wave his left hand out the window, give a big smile, and drive off in a cloud of dust.

Though I sometimes think of him, I don't believe I shall ever see Justin again. Not getting the chance to reminisce with lovers or companions or old friends I meet on journeys is the saddest consequence of travel, and in Africa too many never live to be old friends. I still love Africa and ache to return. I have never seen anything more beautiful than the clouds or stars high above the Great Rift Valley. The land heals its wounds, and its peoples are resilient and eloquent like Justin, whom I will love always.

# ✎ 13    Trying to Stop Water with a Net

*James W. Jones*

For a week or so in April 1989 Hans Paul Verhoef's face was well-known from news stories and television interviews in the United States and the Netherlands, his home country. What first attracted me to him was his shock of blond hair and his tall, lanky build. And the leather pants.

We had met in Amsterdam in December 1987 at an international conference on gay studies and contemporary gay issues. I gave a paper on literature about gay men with AIDS, and Hans Paul was attending the conference as part of his work as a civil servant in the city of Delft, responsible for developing policy and outreach to gay men. He came to the session at which I presented because, as he told me later, he wanted to learn about literature dealing with AIDS. The next morning I happened to be standing next to him at an exhibit table, so I struck up a conversation. We talked briefly about the session and how many of the European participants seemed hesitant to participate since the discussion was held in English. He spoke excellent English, however. Since I did not know anyone at the conference, much less in the city, I asked Hans Paul about the bar scene in Amsterdam. Within minutes we had arranged to meet the next evening to go to dinner and then out to the bars. It all happened so fast that I really wasn't sure if we had arranged a tour or made a date. When I saw him in the lobby of the conference center the following morning I was pretty sure it was a date: he was wearing black leather pants.

They added to his appeal not so much because they symbolized a certain kind of sexual desire, but because they were a sign of being European, of being different from my world. I started learning German in high school in Milwaukee about the same time I started coming to terms with being gay. One reason I fell in love with the language, I have come to realize, is that it provided me a kind of mask or other identity that made difference acceptable. Speaking it, even just thinking in the foreign language, was a way to be different while living in the midst of "normality." You couldn't tell by looking at me that I knew German, just as you couldn't tell by looking at me that I was gay (or at least I hoped people couldn't). For me, knowing a foreign language also opened a path to worlds where I could discover who I would want to be. With it I could explore new cultures and meet new people. The "foreign" represents the possibility not just of acceptance, but the possibility of integration, of uniting desire with reality, of dream with everyday life. Beyond the physical attraction to Hans Paul, those are some of the reasons I was drawn to him, just as we always are attracted not just by a person's appearance but also by what the person represents.

Hans Paul had chosen a nearby Chinese restaurant for dinner. Conversation proved surprisingly easy, and we eventually fell into the well-known pattern of gay first-date conversation: When did you come out? Do your parents know? Ever had a long-term relationship? This getting-to-know-you ritual is necessary and has its charms, but today it seems outdated, I think. Hans Paul's coming-out story was an interesting one, though, even by today's jaded standards. Being a university student concentrating on his studies in municipal planning and his involvement in student politics had led a basically asexual life. But one day he became infatuated with a man and, on a Saturday evening, went home with him. When they turned on the Sunday news, Hans Paul heard a report that the student political group of which he was president was claiming to have kidnapped some official. The reporter stated that the police were looking for Hans Paul Verhoef. He became worried when he realized that his alibi would be that he could not have been kidnapping some politician because he had been having sex with a man! Fortunately, it all turned out to be a hoax, but Hans Paul decided that he never wanted to face that fear of exposure again, so he started being open about being gay.

After dinner we did go to a couple bars, including what has become my favorite stop whenever I am in Amsterdam, the Amstel Taveerne. I love it because it is thoroughly Dutch, without any attempt to be "international," which really means American. The atmosphere of Dutch pop music and crowded intimacy creates a friendliness rarely found any more. Hans Paul and I enjoyed our own kind of crowded intimacy, seated close to each other at the bar. Yes, we were indeed on a date.

"I think I am not going back to my mother's tonight," he announced later in the night, and invited himself to my hotel room, which was fine with me. During the conference he was staying with his mother, who lived in a suburb of Amsterdam, because he did not want to commute by train to his apartment in Delft every day. The phone call to tell his mother that he would not be staying with her that night was coded, even though he was out to her.

"Mom, I'm staying out pretty late. There won't be any more buses to Amstelveen, so I'll just head back to Delft."

"But there are night buses that run!"

"Well...they don't run *that* late."

We spent a wonderful night together. The next day was the final day of the conference, and I was leaving the day after that. We packed a lot into that time. I learned that he was involved in a relationship with another man, Frans, who also had a boyfriend, Jan. The relationship between Hans Paul and Frans was what I will call one of "loving friends." They shared an emotional commitment and sexual intimacy, but they were by no means "partners." Jan and Frans were partners, but Jan, too, enjoyed sexual relationships with other men. This was all very modern, even foreign for me, but like many "foreign" things I found it intriguing, not off-putting. Hans Paul made it clear again and again that he enjoyed being with me and was interested in seeing how our budding friendship would play out. He also told me that Frans had recently been diagnosed with AIDS and was talking AZT.

"Are you HIV positive?" I asked.

"I haven't been tested. I don't want to know. I just assume that I am," he told me.

I was not upset by his response—we had been safe. Nor did I find his statements odd; this was a time when many gay men faced discrimination in jobs and housing and from friends and family if it became known that they were positive. At that time being HIV-positive was the equivalent of "having AIDS" in most people's minds. There also were very few treatments. AZT was the only drug available, and the doses were higher and therefore even more toxic than today.

Hans Paul and I spent most of the rest of my time together in Delft. There are people who form relationships largely by doing things together, and there are people who form relationships by talking, by telling their stories and discovering the other person's story. We belonged to the latter group. I cannot remember everything we talked about, but I do remember the feeling of it being right, secure, not love—much too soon for that—but trust and friendship and happiness. When I asked him what he thought would happen once I left he told me, "I think this is the end of a beginning, but not the beginning of an end."

I described in such detail how we got to know each other because so many of the elements from that story reappear in what happened later. We stayed in contact by mail and phone. (This was before everyone used e-mail.) In March 1988 I spent the week of my spring break from teaching visiting him in Delft, and our friendship intensified.

That summer, Hans Paul made his first trip to the United States. In his three weeks I introduced him to the various sides of U.S. life: the small-town world of the city where I live and work, the metropolitan life of Chicago and San Francisco, and my network of friends in Madison, Wisconsin, where I used to spend every summer. He enjoyed it all tremendously, experiencing in person the images—and stereotypes ("They are so fat!")—that he had previously known only from American films and television series. His English, like that of most Dutch people, was excellent, but sometimes I would be surprised at the extent of his vocabulary. Early on he turned to me as we were lying in bed and said, "I like to cuddle." I wondered where he had learned that word. Surely even progressive schoolbooks in liberal Holland did not go that far? "I learned it from a story in an American porn magazine." As a foreign language teacher I could well appreciate the many modes of vocabulary acquisition.

By the end of his visit our relationship had deepened, evolving into a variation on the kind of loving friendship he had with Frans. We continued to write and call each other, and even exchanged audio tapes we had made, telling the other about what was happening in our lives. In the fall of 1988 Hans Paul developed a series of illnesses, and it came as little surprise when he told me that he had been diagnosed with AIDS. In late September Frans died. For a time Hans Paul lost his way. He became depressed and took short-term disability leave.

Soon, however, he found a new goal in life. He became active in local and then in national public policy debates regarding the issues of HIV prevention and people with AIDS (PWA). Because of this work he was sent to participate in a major gay health conference held in San Francisco in April 1989. He knew that the INS (Immigration and Naturalization Service), using regulations enacted in the Reagan years, sometimes refused entry to openly gay tourists and that PWA in particular could well be sent back on the next plane if customs agents discovered the person's health status. Before leaving the Netherlands Hans Paul asked me for information on legal aid, just in case this might happen to him. I told him about Lambda Legal, but I doubted anything would happen when he changed planes in Minneapolis. He told me he would call me once he arrived in San Francisco so that we could finalize plans for the rest of his trip, which included visits in Madison and Mount Pleasant before a week in New York City.

When the phone rang early on the evening of April 2, 1989, I assumed Hans Paul was calling from San Francisco. Instead, it was a lesbian friend of mine from Duluth, Minnesota. In somber tones she asked, "Have you heard about Hans Paul?" The way she asked I thought he had died on the plane!

"He's in jail in Minneapolis. I just heard on NPR." She did not know where he was being held, but told me parts of the story that television reports on CNN and the network news fleshed out. In response to the standard question from the customs agent, "Why are you visiting the United States?" Hans Paul told the truth and mentioned the conference. The name of the conference raised two red flags: The Eleventh National Lesbian and Gay Health Conference and Seventh AIDS Forum. The agent pressed for more information, and Hans Paul showed him the conference invitation along with his application for a scholarship to help pay the cost of attending. Such scholarships were only available to people with AIDS.

"Do you have AIDS?" asked the agent. Again, Hans Paul told the truth. The agent then informed him that the United States considers AIDS a "dangerous, contagious disease," and that he therefore had two options: to return to Amsterdam on the next available flight or to apply for a travel waiver. Hans Paul refused to leave. He was put in handcuffs, fingerprinted, and placed in the county jail. Using his one phone call, he called Lambda Legal in New York City. They contacted a law firm in Minneapolis, and one of their lawyers started proceedings to obtain the travel waiver.

The process stretched out for five days. After spending two days in the local jail, wearing handcuffs and an orange jumpsuit ("Hideous!" according to Hans Paul), the Minnesota corrections commissioner intervened and had him moved to the hospital ward of the state prison. This was a maximum security prison. As Hans Paul described, "You only get there if you have killed at least one person." But being in the hospital ward allowed him to be treated more as a "guest" than a prisoner. In the county jail he had been treated just like all the other inmates. Here he had privacy, wore his own clothes, and was given unrestricted access to hold interviews and receive phone calls. The lawyers got the word out to the national media, and soon Hans Paul was giving interviews to radio, television, and newspaper reporters from the Netherlands, the United States, and even other foreign countries. The pressure was building on INS to release him. After a two-and-a-half-hour hearing on his fourth day of incarceration, the four regional INS officials recommended the waiver be granted, but the authorities in Washington, DC, refused to do so.

Imagine being in prison, even as a budding media celebrity, in a foreign country in a city where you know no one. This was an enormous psychological stress for him. His lawyer was very helpful and the people in the prison, officials and prisoners alike, were extremely kind. They were embarrassed at the way their country was treating him. A local woman, whose son had died of AIDS, brought him homemade cookies. I felt so bad that I could not really do anything, much less be close to him. I tried to contact him but succeeded only in sending him a message via one of the lawyers, so that he would at least know I was trying to reach him. When I asked him later on why he went through this ordeal, adding this stress to that of being HIV positive, he told me he believed it was time for someone to draw attention to the idiocy of American policy toward people with AIDS in order to get it changed. The policy of keeping foreign nationals with HIV out of the United States, he said, was like trying to stop water with a net; it was futile and missed the point of how HIV is transmitted. In addition, he himself contradicted the prevailing view of PWA as weak and sickly: "Thousands of people with AIDS could see someone with AIDS standing up for his rights. And I look rather healthy, so there's another image."

The next afternoon, a formal hearing was held in court before a judge and in the presence of many media representatives. Again Hans Paul had to testify about very personal issues. In the questioning by the INS lawyer the modes of HIV transmission became central, and inadvertently comic, points. In his luggage the customs agents had found not only the conference invitation and his AZT medication but also several objects that they euphemistically termed "sexual paraphernalia" (a dildo, nipple clamps, a cock ring, and condoms and lube). Since the U.S. law was supposedly intended to prevent infection of American citizens by foreigners, the INS lawyer pressed Hans Paul on the stand to say that he intended to have sex while in the United States. To the INS these items were indications of that intent. He could have claimed that as an AIDS educator (which was part of his job in Delft) he brought the items as visual aids for his talk at the conference. Instead, he again told the truth, but did so by forcing the INS lawyer to be more precise.

"What do you mean 'have sex'?" he asked. "Do you mean kissing? Do you mean embracing? Do you mean cuddling? Mutual masturbation?" The lawyer tried to avoid a precise response to Hans Paul's questions, but finally turned beet red from embarrassment and demanded that the judge order Hans Paul to answer.

"Everyone knows very well what 'to have sex' means, Judge!"

Surprisingly, the judge agreed with Hans Paul, telling the lawyer that there are many ways to be intimate and that not all would possibly transmit HIV, so he would have to be more explicit in his questions: just which methods did he mean? Too embarrassed to do so, the lawyer grunted his frustration and ended the questioning.

The judge granted a thirty-day travel waiver, but Hans Paul had to promise he would not engage in any sexual activity that could transmit HIV. With a twinkle in his eye he agreed. The Minnesota AIDS Project also put up the money for the $10,000 bond required for his release; supposedly, the money would be needed to pay his medical expenses should he require health care while in the United States. The INS tried to appeal the ruling, but it was denied on a technicality. They had missed the five p.m. filing deadline. The state corrections commissioner took Hans Paul out for a pancake breakfast the following morning, and then he finally boarded a plane and flew to San Francisco.

By then the conference was over, but his moment of fame was still going strong. Upon arriving in San Francisco he was greeted with a bouquet of flowers and a limousine, provided by the mayor who had declared it "Hans Paul Verhoef Day." More interviews followed, and he was able to meet with some of the conference participants and organizers, so he did not miss out entirely on what was to have been the purpose of his trip. From San Francisco Hans Paul flew to Madison, where he spent several days with my friends whom he had met the previous summer. There were more interviews, but this was also a needed time to decompress from all the stress and attention of the previous week and a half. Finally, he came to Mount Pleasant, and I had a chance to speak with him in person about the enormous adventure he had been on. I was amazed at his strength and at his calmness about it. I realized again that those were some of the chief qualities that had drawn me so strongly to him.

He also remained the AIDS educator during our days together. Michael, a young man whom I had dated seriously, had been diagnosed

HIV positive just a few weeks prior to Hans Paul's visit. He was having a hard time dealing with this new reality, and Hans Paul spent several afternoons alone with him, talking about what it means—and does not mean—to live with HIV. He even presented to Michael the pair of black leather pants he had brought along on the trip.

"I think they will look good on you," he told him. "Besides, my suitcase is getting too heavy with all the things people have been giving me." They were the pants he had worn the night of our first date. Seeing them here, in my apartment in Mount Pleasant, and on Michael, a boyfriend who had become, like Hans Paul, a loving friend, seemed to close a circle.

From Mount Pleasant Hans Paul traveled to Washington, DC, where national gay rights organizations had set up meetings with important politicians (his favorite was Senator Kennedy) and more interviews with various print and television reporters. When he returned to the Netherlands at the end of his thirty days he at first found it difficult to cope with the loss of celebrity status. I sent him copies of articles about him from various newspapers and magazines, and he told me the coverage in the Dutch media was even more extensive and enraged. It was a challenge to return to dealing with public policy at the local level after what he had experienced in America. Soon he took a medical leave from his job. Although he had developed Kaposi's sarcoma, he was not seriously ill. Taking this leave enabled him to devote his energy full time to AIDS-prevention work and to improving public policy on the national level for PWA.

In early 1990 he became the first chairman of the national organization for PWA, the HIV-Vereinigung (Union). He thrived in this work and met many interesting people. At one meeting in Amsterdam, even Queen Beatrix attended. She was seated right next to Hans Paul. "Two queens at the same table!" he reported with his characteristic burst of laughter. "Once I happened to look down and I saw that she had taken off her shoes and tucked one leg up underneath her, just like she was sitting on a couch at home listening to the prince talk about something!"

As the year progressed, the disease began taking a toll. He had respiratory problems, then stomach problems, and was hospitalized for a period in the spring. I was planning a trip to see him in May before going on to do research in Germany. He encouraged me to come and even bought us tickets to a major exhibition of Van Gogh's paintings. I offered to postpone, or at least to stay in a hotel, but he refused to hear of it. He did warn me that I would find him looking quite different, as he had lost weight and more lesions had appeared. For me the main thing was to be with him; I didn't care how he looked.

His warning was well taken, but still I was a bit shocked when he met me at the airport. His height made him easy to find, but he looked frail, and even the bright blond hair had faded to match the ashen tone of his skin. When we greeted each other he smiled with still a good portion of the broad sly grin I knew from our first meeting. I could tell that he had trepidations, too. How would I react? I had wondered that myself during the long flight from Detroit, but when I put my arms around him and kissed him I felt the anxiety slip away, from me and from him. Our feelings of love and friendship had not changed, but the situation had, and we would just have to face it.

We drove back to Delft and went grocery shopping. He even had some coupons, which he knew are one of my favorite parts of shopping. That evening I offered to cook or to get takeout, but he insisted on making dinner. This was typical of our exchanges in the five days I spent with him: I would offer to help but he would say no, thanks. Finally I realized he wanted to prove to himself even more than to me that he was still able to do these everyday tasks. One of his few concessions to the disease was that he used a wheelchair when we saw the Van Gogh exhibit. I had trouble steering it on the cobblestones as we went to and from the car, veering this way and that, into and out of the line of traffic, but Hans Paul just laughed at the predicament.

One evening we had a long conversation about his future, which he knew would not be a long one. He talked about his plans for his death. Having trained as a civil engineer, the plans were precise and detailed. During this visit I met the two people most involved in his daily care, and he told me they would notify people, including me, of his death. The cremation and memorial service were also set. All I could do was tell him, "I wish I could help you. I wish I could be here with you." We embraced for a long time. What else was there to do?

That night I had an extremely vivid dream. Hans Paul and I were having fun, sitting outside under a starry sky, joking and talking. He looked like he did when he visited me the summer of 1988, sexy and full of life. He went into the house to get ready for bed but I stayed outside. The next thing I knew there was thunder and lightning and it started raining, but the rain was not raindrops, it was little bits of fire, and the fire-rain set the house on fire. I ran to the house, yelling for Hans Paul to get out, but got no response. Maybe he was asleep. I tried every door and window, but they all were locked and I couldn't break them in. The firefighters came, but by now the house was engulfed in flame, with fire shooting out of the windows and doors. I screamed at them that Hans Paul was inside, but they told me it was too late. I woke up terrified. My heart was pounding, and at first I was not even sure where I was. I went quietly from the guest room, where I was sleeping, across the hall to Hans Paul's bedroom and checked to see if he was alright. He was sleeping. It was three a.m. I sat awake the rest of the night. At breakfast he could tell something was wrong. That dream had not only scared me, it had disturbed me. I told him about it and he gave me a long, sympathetic look. Then he quietly stated, "You can't save me, Jim."

As I left for Germany a couple days later I thought of Hans Paul's words to me when I had asked him about our relationship in December of 1987. Then he had told me, "I think this is the end of a beginning, but not the beginning of an end." Now it was most probably the beginning of the end for us, for him. We both knew that this was the last time we would see each other in person, unless some miracle happened. Two months later he died. It was July 23, 1990. Hans Paul Verhoef was thirty-three years old.

In Madison my friends and I held a memorial service for him. We shared memories of both the personal and the political sides of his life. Among many moments, I remembered our drive from Michigan to Wisconsin and how we sang along to the tape he'd made of Connie Francis's greatest hits. Our international relationship meant a lot to us both. I felt that I had helped to open up a new world for him: the world of America where being gay carries such a different meaning than it does in Europe or in the Netherlands. He also taught me a very valuable lesson. For Hans Paul, the experience of AIDS—like the experience of being gay—was one that must be shared. That is why he took the drastically public step of going to jail: to make it ineradicably clear that we are all in this together.

I still think of him fondly. When I become frustrated with the slow pace of change or the idiocy of public policy on homosexuality I look at that photo of him in those black leather pants, with his thatch of bright blond hair and a mischievous grin on his face. He gives me hope.

# About the Editor

Michael Luongo's travel writing has appeared in *Condé Nast Traveler, The New York Times,* the *Chicago Tribune, National Geographic Traveler, Town & Country Travel, The Advocate, PlanetOut,* and *The Out Traveler,* among many others, as well as other publications and Web sites. His writing on gay travel runs from the academic to the erotic. In 1996 he pioneered bringing gay tourism into the academic world by co-authoring an article in the *Annals of Tourism Research.* In 2002 he also co-edited *Gay Tourism: Culture, Identity and Sex* (Continuum Press, 2002), the first academic book on the gay travel industry. He is the Senior Editor for Haworth Press's book series Out in the World.

Michael has been to more than seventy-five countries and all seven continents, and has lived on three of them. Geographically, his favorite parts of the world are Latin America and the Middle East and Muslim nations. He has written more from a gay travel perspective on these regions than has perhaps any other gay American. Of utmost importance to Michael is looking beyond the stereotypical gay circuit travel and looking at destinations that challenge Western notions of homosexuality. His most challenging and shocking work in that regard has been that regarding post–9/11 Middle East and Afghanistan, some of which will appear in his upcoming Haworth book tentatively titled *Gay Travels in The Muslim World.* Michael is a native of New Jersey, growing up near the shore in Springsteen country. He now lives in upper Manhattan. As a child, his parents never took him anywhere that could not be driven to and back from in a day, but they gave him many books about exotic places, and he vowed at an early age to see each and every one of them.

Michael is dedicating the collection to L.F. and L.W., two friends in Buenos Aires who found love overseas and settled in Buenos Aires, and who will soon celebrate 25 years together. In addition, he is co-dedicating the collection to M.S. Hunter, the author of "Samoa Memories" and to Richard D. Thompson who wrote "Blue Asia." Both of these men died during the editing of this book, and special permission was received from their families to ensure their last works were published.

Visit Michael at www.michaelluongo.com for updates on his travel writing and photography adventures.

# Contributors

**Des Ariel** lives a quiet life with his own thoughts. He travels sometimes, but not much anymore, except to Africa. His story "Twelve Days in a Week" recently appeared in Foreign Affairs (2004, Cleis Press), but he has written under another guise. He has published journalism, essays, and fiction in various erotica anthologies and online. Novels take a long time to write and publish; story collections even longer.

**Ken Baehr** is originally from Western New York but now calls Manhattan's East Village his home. In his free time he enjoys coaching miniature golf, bloodletting, and Fresca. He may be reached at ken.baehr@gmail.com.

"To Jennifer, for the ceaseless love and support. This is for you, babybird."

**Thomas Bradbury** is a pseudonym for a New York travel agent who specializes in Turkey. He changed his name to protect the innocent, and the guilty.

"I dedicate this story to all my wonderful friends in Turkey, who have renewed and changed my life in ways I could never imagine."

**Richard Burnett** is Editor at Large of the Montreal weekly alternative magazine Hour, where he writes Canada's first and only national queer-issues column "Three Dollar Bill." His writing (under the names Bugs Burnett and Richard Burnett) has appeared in national and international publications, he speaks regularly at universities and conferences, cofounded the Montreal chapter of the National Gay and Lesbian Journalists Association, and was one of the original organizers

*Looking for Love in Faraway Places*
© 2007 The Haworth Press, Inc. All rights reserved.
doi:10.1300/5366_15

of Divers/Cité, Montreal's Gay Pride organization, from 1993 to 1996. You can read "Three Dollar Bill" by surfing to www.hour.ca.

"I'd like to dedicate the piece to Justin."

**Dayton Estes** is a North Carolinian by birth. He has taught German literature and philology at East Carolina University and Pfeiffer University in Misenheimer, North Carolina. He has published in his own field of Germanics, but is new at writing fiction. His stories are included in *Rebel Yell: Stories by Contemporary Southern Gay Authors* (Harrington Park Press, 2001), *Rebel Yell 2: More Stories of Contemporary Southern Gay Men* (Harrington Park Press, 2002), *Between the Palms: A Collection of Gay Travel Erotica* (Harrington Park Press, 2004), *Best Gay Erotica 2004* (Cleis Press, 2003), and *Wet Nightmares, Wet Dreams* (STARBooks Press, 2005). He is retired and lives in Oak Island, North Carolina. You can e-mail him at dayton32.1@Netzero.com.

**Marc J. Heft** is a native New Yorker who currently resides in Lower Manhattan. He has contributed short stories to several anthologies, including *Latin Lovers: True Stories of Latin Men in Love* (Painted Leaf Press, 1999), *Men Seeking Men* (Painted Leaf Press, 1998), and *Boy Meets Boy* (Saint Martins Press, 1999). Marc is also a photo enthusiast who has had photographs published in *Think*, a popular lifestyle magazine in Prague. A world traveler who has visited more than fifty countries on six continents, he is thrilled to share his experiences with the gay community. Marc hopes to continue traveling to exotic, faraway places, including a trip to Antarctica—he feels it would be rude to leave out just one continent. He can be contacted at Marcheft@hotmail.com.

"I would like to dedicate this story to my fellow travelers who venture out into the world with nothing more than a guidebook, a backpack, and a smile, but who hopefully return with memories that will enrich their lives forever."

**M. S. Hunter,** known to his friends as Max, with a real name of Frank A. Rhuland Jr., died during the making of this book. This Massachusetts native did two of the things he enjoyed to the end: he wrote and he traveled, dying on July 2, 2004, in Honduras. With the help of his sister Amy Rhuland Davis we were able to include his wonderful, sexy but sensitive, and funny work in this collection. I am forever grateful to her, and am honored as an editor. When Max submitted this story to me, he had this comment, "Looking through my old pictures taken during that time in Samoa, it occurred to me that enough years have passed so that no one still living is apt to be offended or embarrassed by my revelations. Of course, some admirers of the late Margaret Mead would probably have a fit, but that's just too bad." Whether such people are offended or not, I am happy to have Max's work in this collection.

**James W. Jones** is Professor of German and Chair of the Department of Foreign Languages, Literatures, and Cultures at Central Michigan University in Mount Pleasant, Michigan. His book *We of the Third Sex: Literary Representations of Homosexuality in Wilhelmine Germany* (Peter Lang Publishing, 1990) is a comprehensive history of German gay and lesbian literature from 1870 to 1918. He has published articles on German and American AIDS discourses as well as on German and American gay films. He has also written extensively on the persecution of gays by the Nazis, and was the first to translate Charlotte von Mahlsdorf's telling of her story "I Am My Own Woman" in *Gay Voices from East Germany* (Indiana University Press, 1991).

"To Hans Paul Verhoef, a dear friend and fellow fighter." (Hans Paul Verhoef, 1957-1990, was an AIDS activist and educator at the local level in Delft and the national level in the Netherlands.)

**Morris Kafka** was born in Brooklyn, New York, the second of three children and the first son to an English professor and her fashion engineer husband. He was raised in various New Jersey suburbs, moving to New Brunswick, where he still resides, when he was a student. He graduated Rutgers College with an art history degree. He has spent the past sixteen years restoring an 1889 Victorian house. He has published in various Rutgers University journals and is the author of a column on old-house living. He volunteers extensively in the community. He is a founding archivist of the New Jersey LGBT archives, housed at Rutgers.

"To My Mother, for her consistent support in countless ways."

**Michael Mele** is a traveler, a writer, and the director of Il Chiostro, Inc., which produces arts-related workshops in Italy. He has written a children's book titled *A Gift for the Contessa* (Pelican Publishing company, 1997, with illustrations by Ron Paolillo), contributed a short story to the gay travel anthology *Between the Palms: A Collection of Gay Travel Erotica* (Harrington Park Press, 2004), and has written several articles about the pleasures of tea for *Tea: A Magazine*. Michael's poetry was published in 2003 in the Gay and Lesbian Review-Worldwide.

He dedicates this story to Marcelo, a sweet partner in a tango dance.

**Gabriel Schael** lives in Los Angeles with his Spanish partner. He is a Partner in DaSi Tours, a gay and lesbian travel company that specializes in Spain and Spanish-speaking countries. He has written and directed two short films, the horror short *Bait* and *Rocket Queens,* a dark comedy in which a gay basher finds the tables turned when he messes with the wrong couple. He is currently at work on his next project. Though he no longer needs to pursue love in faraway places, he highly recommends it to others. In his spare time he counts his blessings and prays for dual citizenship.

He is thrilled to dedicate his first published piece to the one that made it all happen.

**Richard D. Thompson** was raised on a cattle farm in Idaho. He lived twelve years in New York City, mainly as a journalist. Ten years ago he moved to the San Francisco Bay Area to become a teacher to Latino elementary students. He traveled often to Europe and Latin America, and spent a year crossing Iran, Afghanistan, Pakistan, India, and Nepal, and spent several months in East Asia. He had a degree in philosophy from Reed College and a master's degree in journalism from Columbia University. He was a retired PWA and spent as much time as he could working on travel stories. Richard died during the making of this book. His last trip was to Alaska. He sent many e-mails telling me of how happy he was to be making a voyage to that part of the world. He passed away on March 9, 2005, and his traveling up until the end of his life should be an inspiration to us all. It is with his mother Gloria Martin's permission that we include his last piece of writing in this collection.

## Order a copy of this book with this form or online at:
http://www.haworthpress.com/store/product.asp?sku=5366

# LOOKING FOR LOVE IN FARAWAY PLACES
## Tales of Gay Men's Romance Overseas

_____ in hardbound at $22.95 (ISBN-13: 978-1-56023-697-9; ISBN-10: 1-56023-697-3)

_____ in softbound at $14.95 (ISBN-13: 978-1-56023-539-2; ISBN-10: 1-56023-539-X)

*150 pages*

Or order online and use special offer code HEC25 in the shopping cart.

COST OF BOOKS_____

☐ **BILL ME LATER:** (Bill-me option is good on US/Canada/Mexico orders only; not good to jobbers, wholesalers, or subscription agencies.)

POSTAGE & HANDLING_____
*(US: $4.00 for first book & $1.50 for each additional book)*
*(Outside US: $5.00 for first book & $2.00 for each additional book)*

☐ Check here if billing address is different from shipping address and attach purchase order and billing address information.

Signature_____

SUBTOTAL_____

☐ **PAYMENT ENCLOSED:** $_____

IN CANADA: ADD 6% GST_____

☐ **PLEASE CHARGE TO MY CREDIT CARD.**

STATE TAX_____
*(NJ, NY, OH, MN, CA, IL, IN, PA, & SD residents, add appropriate local sales tax)*

☐ Visa ☐ MasterCard ☐ AmEx ☐ Discover
☐ Diner's Club ☐ Eurocard ☐ JCB

Account # _____

**FINAL TOTAL**_____
*(If paying in Canadian funds, convert using the current exchange rate, UNESCO coupons welcome)*

Exp. Date_____

Signature_____

Prices in US dollars and subject to change without notice.

NAME_____

INSTITUTION_____

ADDRESS_____

CITY_____

STATE/ZIP_____

COUNTRY_____ COUNTY (NY residents only)_____

TEL_____ FAX_____

E-MAIL_____

May we use your e-mail address for confirmations and other types of information? ☐ Yes ☐ No
We appreciate receiving your e-mail address and fax number. Haworth would like to e-mail or fax special discount offers to you, as a preferred customer. **We will never share, rent, or exchange your e-mail address or fax number.** We regard such actions as an invasion of your privacy.

*Order From Your Local Bookstore or Directly From*
**The Haworth Press, Inc.**
10 Alice Street, Binghamton, New York 13904-1580 • USA
TELEPHONE: 1-800-HAWORTH (1-800-429-6784) / Outside US/Canada: (607) 722-5857
FAX: 1-800-895-0582 / Outside US/Canada: (607) 771-0012
E-mail to: orders@haworthpress.com

**For orders outside US and Canada,** you may wish to order through your local
sales representative, distributor, or bookseller.
For information, see http://haworthpress.com/distributors

*(Discounts are available for individual orders in US and Canada only, not booksellers/distributors.)*

PLEASE PHOTOCOPY THIS FORM FOR YOUR PERSONAL USE.
http://www.HaworthPress.com                                          BOF06